**THE MINNESOTA
CRIME WAVE PRESENTS**

Fifteen Tales of Murder, Mayhem, and Malice

from the Land of

Minnesota Nice

**THE MINNESOTA
CRIME WAVE PRESENTS**

Fifteen Tales of Murder, Mayhem, and Malice

from the Land of

Minnesota Nice

NODIN PRESS

Library of Congress Cataloging-in-Publication Data

Fifteen tales of murder, mayhem, and malice from the land of Minnesota nice / Minnesota Crime Wave.
p. cm.
ISBN 978-1-935666-43-1
1. Minnesota--Fiction. 2. Detective and mystery stories, American.
I. Minnesota Crime Wave (Group)
PN6120.95.D45F54 2012
808.83'872--dc23

2012027825

printed in the United States
Cover and layout: John Toren

Nodin Press
530 North 3rd Street
Suite 120,
Minneapolis, MN
55401

Contents

Introduction

Pete Hautman

It is true: Minnesota folks are infuriatingly nice. Also, they won't stop talking about the weather. Is it any wonder a few of us snap?

My first (failed) effort to write a book was the story of two men who attempt to write a novel together. They take themselves to a small cabin on a remote lake in northern Minnesota. As they struggle to write, winter sets in, and reality takes its leave. Their book becomes increasingly violent as their mutual antipathy grows. Soon, the story they are trying to tell becomes indistinguishable from the lives they are living. Of course, everybody ends up dead at the end, because winters in Minnesota are long and cold, and because I didn't know how else to end it.

Minnesotans are contrarians. Always have been. Consider the early immigrants who chose to settle here, from the rice-harvesting Ojibwe to the lutefisk-eating Swedish pioneers. With more than two billion acres to choose from, they went for the coldest, rockiest land they could find, named their football team after an extinct race of Nordic warriors who never got within a thousand miles of the place, and elected a professional wrestler for governor.

It is no coincidence that there are a lot of writers in Minnesota. Contrariness and cabin fever breeds writers. Also, based on what you will find in these pages, it breeds murderers, thieves, and psychopaths. Not that we have an exclusive on bad behavior—Wisconsin has several legs up on the whole cannibal thing—but there is a sort of North Dakota-meets-Iowa smiling bleakness available here in Minnesota that manifests itself as suppressed rage. Cut somebody off in traffic and you won't get road rage, you will get the Minnesota Look—the face of a cat depositing a nuisance on your pillow. For those unversed in the silent language of the Look, allow me to translate: *I kill you with my thoughts.*

The fifteen Minnesota writers featured in this volume are looking at you and smiling. They would like you to Have a Nice Day.

Fifteen Tales of Murder, Mayhem, and Malice

from the Land of

Minnesota Nice

Marilyn Victor, along with Michael Allen Mallory, is co-author of *Death Roll* and *Killer Instinct*, which feature mystery's first zookeeper sleuth, Snake Jones. Snake Jones uses her knowledge of animals to solve murders and offers a unique perspective of what goes on behind the scenes of zoos and wildlife parks. Her short stories have appeared in the anthologies *Once Upon A Crime*, *Deadly Treats*, and *Writes of Spring*. She volunteers for a local pet rescue group and shares her home with a special needs Maltese and a noisy cockatiel.

This Old House

Marilyn Victor

As usual, Justine's sister was sitting on the third floor balcony of the nursing home, binoculars pressed against her shrewd eyes, watching the world that stretched out beneath her.

"I wish you could come out and see this," Esther said, looking back at her sister. "I can see the backyard of the house. That old oak tree barely topped the roof when we were kids. Now look at it."

Justine didn't have to step onto the balcony to know it afforded a clear view of the house their parents built after settling in central Minnesota. It hadn't been their first house, of course. They were as poor as dirt when they emigrated from Sweden, and barely survived their first Minnesota winter. But they had worked hard and eventually owned the biggest house in town.

Justine pressed her back against the doorjamb of the French doors, refusing to take a step onto the balcony. She didn't share her sister's enthusiasm for heights.

Esther unlocked the wheels of her wheelchair and used her feet to pull herself toward the doorway. Her hands were too crippled with arthritis to use the wheel's push rim. "There's a family of birds building a nest inside that old tree house Papa built for us."

Built for you, Justine thought. Father had never done anything for her.

Justine took a step back from the doorway, watching as Esther struggled to maneuver the wheelchair across the balcony's uneven floor. To Justine, the flooring appeared to have a downward slope toward the balcony's edge. She imagined her sister rolling backward and over that edge. She, of course, would be too scared to move.

"I get her for you," one of the nurses said, brushing past Justine, her accent hinting of a life spent closer to the equator. She pushed Esther into the sunny visiting room and toward a table next to a large birdcage that housed a trio of cockatiels.

"Not there," Justine said, her face draining of color. She hated birds.

Her face full of disapproval, the nurse steered her patient toward a window with a beautiful view of the park, but Justine stopped her again.

"In the corner, Mercy," Esther suggested sweetly. "Poor Justine gets very nervous around windows. It's the height, you know."

Once they were settled at the table and Mercy had brought them a delicate china pot of coffee and a plate of chocolate chip cookies, Justine tried to relax. She hated sitting with all these old people. It was true, she was five years older than her sister, but she didn't feel her age. All of these people wasting away, waiting to die, scared the hell out of her. She didn't want to end up like one of them. When she died she was going to be on a warm, sandy beach, not sharing a room with another old geezer in a place like this. The only thing stopping her was the lack of money.

"Have a cookie," Esther offered, picking the largest one from the plate. "They're fresh. I could smell them baking this morning. It reminded me of Mama."

"You know I can't eat chocolate," Justine snapped. She shouldn't have to remind her. Justine had been allergic to chocolate since she was three years old.

"More for me, then." Esther chomped happily on her cookie, waggling her fingers at an orderly that walked by and smiled at her. "Everyone here is so nice, but I would really prefer to be at home, Justine."

"How would you get on, what with all those stairs?" Justine asked, not for the first time. This line of conversation had been going on for the two months her sister had been living at Happy Heights Nursing Home. "Who would make sure you take all of your medications? I can't do all of that for you, Esther. You know that." And she didn't want to.

"Mama could come and live with me."

Justine rolled her eyes. "Mother has been dead for fifteen years."

Esther's smile turned downward. "I saw Mama this morning."

She set her coffee cup down with a sigh. "And how did she look? She must be what? One hundred and ten by now?" Her sister's recent forgetfulness had been funny at first, now it was simply irritating.

Esther let the remark pass with an annoyed sigh. "We could hire someone. We always had someone around to help with the chores."

"You don't have any money to pay for help. If it weren't for county aide, you wouldn't be able to stay here either—unless I sold the house." She crossed her fingers, hoping this time she could get her sister to agree.

Esther tapped a thickened fingernail against the table. "The house is half mine."

"It's also half mine," Justine reminded her. "And I'm going to sell it."

Esther's eyes widened, real fear in them. "But, what about Papa's money?"

"What money?" Justine smirked. "Don't tell me you believe all those stupid rumors."

Justine could sense the other residents in the room leaning toward them. A small town had thousands of ears, even if most of them were wearing hearing aids. Wouldn't they all like to hear there really was money hidden in the old house?

Esther sipped at her coffee, her wrinkled face serious. "Father doesn't like banks. After the crash he was more determined than ever not to let one red cent out of his sight."

"Father is dead, Esther."

"Oh, you think everyone is dead. What am I going to tell him when he gets here?" Cookie crumbs sputtered from Esther's mouth.

Justine pushed herself back from the table to avoid the cookie missiles that seemed to be aimed right at her. "Maybe you can ask him where he hid all this money."

Esther shook her head as if her sister were the most thick-headed creature she knew. "It was when we did the remodeling. Papa had a tin box he hid in the wall, remember?"

"Which remodeling project would that be?" she asked, breaking off a small piece of cookie and inspecting it for hints of chocolate. "Father was always tearing down walls and putting up new ones. He was never satisfied."

"It was a big box. I painted it red for him so he wouldn't lose it."

Justine paused, the scrap of cookie halfway to her lips. There were days when her sister seemed to be off in Lalaland, and then there were days when she was as sharp as a tack, remembering the patent leather shoes with the white bows Father had bought her for her fifth birthday, over seventy years ago. It was quite possible Esther could remember seeing her father hide something in the walls. No bank had ever turned up any hidden accounts, and Justine had barraged them all for information on her father's supposedly vast fortune.

Justine repeated her question. "Which project, Esther?"

When she got a dull look from her sister, she tried another tactic, speaking to her sister as is she was a small child. "If we could find the money, Esther, you could come home and have your old room back. We could put one of those electric chairs on the stairway, one that carries you upstairs. Would you like that?"

Esther clapped her hands together. "Aunt Selma had one. She used to let us ride up and down the stairs whenever we came to visit. It was so much fun, wasn't it?"

"Right up until you pushed me off the top of the stairs." Justine wondered if that had been the start of all her fears. She didn't like things that went up and down. Carnival rides, escalators, elevators. Ladders. She preferred both feet planted firmly on the ground.

"I did not push you." Esther rested a gnarled hand gently on top of Justine's. "I was two. You were seven. It was an accident."

Justine pulled her hand away, not wanting to think about it. "If we found the money, you could move back to the house."

Esther shrugged and added yet another sugar cube to her coffee. "It's in the attic. Don't you remember when he built Mama a sewing room up there?"

"The room he built so he could lock her in when he was drinking?"

Esther pursed her lips into a sour pout. "He did no such thing. Mama got stuck in there once, that's all."

Justine dismissed Esther's excuse with a wave of her hand.

"There's nothing in the attic. It was cleaned completely out after Mother died."

This time Esther didn't challenge Justine about their mother being dead. Instead she clutched the coffee cup in both hands and brought it up to her lips, a sly look in her eyes. "No one would ever clean behind the insulation, would they?"

Justine's eyes narrowed as she studied her sister. If Esther was right, there could be thousands of dollars hidden in the attic. Maybe millions. If she was wrong, there were always ways Justine could rush her sister toward those pearly gates. Then the house could be sold and she'd be on a Mexican beach the next time a blizzard swept through the state. Either way she was a winner.

"What you watching out there, Miss Esther?" Mercy asked as she came to tell the old woman her sister was back again. As usual Esther was sitting on the edge of the balcony, the binoculars aimed at the old house she used to live in.

"Just some crows. They're very smart, you know."

"Your sister is becoming as big a nuisance as them crows. This be the third time she be here this week. What stories you telling her now, Miss Esther?" She winked at her charge and wheeled her out of the late spring sunshine and back to the table in the corner where her sister Justine waited for her.

Esther frowned, taking in her sister's reddened face and hands. "Did you find a hornet's nest?" Justine's face looked as if she had taken a steel wool pad to it.

Justine shook her head. "It was that damned insulation," she complained, scratching at her reddened hands.

"Mercy can get you something for that, if you like," Esther offered with an overly sweet smile.

Justine quit her scratching and glared at her. "You know I'm allergic to all those fancy creams of yours. They'd only make me itch more."

Esther sighed. "Poor dear. You're allergic to everything. Papa always said it was a miracle you could get through the day without breaking into a rash."

Father had never had anything nice to say about Justine. It

didn't matter that she was the prettiest and the smartest, it was always Esther who got her parent's attention. Why, they wouldn't even get rid of that damned cat Esther carried with her everywhere when Justine started sneezing around it. The only thing she ever got was criticism; as if she could help she was allergic to things. All Esther had to do was smile that sweet simpering smile of hers and they'd do anything she wanted.

"Papa's coming to visit this afternoon," Esther announced happily. "He'll want some of that money he hid behind the bathroom wall."

Justine almost began her litany of father being dead, than stopped herself. Her hands were itching like mad and she fought to keep them clenched tightly in her lap.

"You said the money was behind the insulation in the attic."

"I said no such thing."

"I guess he'll have to go look for it himself, then," Justine snapped, wondering how she let Esther drag her into this fantasy. There was no money. There never had been.

"Don't be absurd. He hasn't taken a step in that house since Mama tossed him out."

"Father got drunk and fell out of the tree house. He broke his fool neck."

"Shush!" Esther leaned forward and lowered her voice. "Don't you be bad-mouthing Papa. He put that money under the bathroom window and he said he's going to buy that new car I want."

"Car?" Justine glanced meaningfully at the wheelchair. "How are you going to drive a car?" This inability to be aware of her physical limits was what had landed her sister in the nursing home in the first place.

"I've got my license. I can drive whenever I want."

Mercy had arrived unseen to their table, beaming a wide smile at them. She placed a tender hand on the old woman's arm. "You need to take your medications," she said, handing Esther a glass of water and a small white cup that rattled with pills.

Esther shook her head. "I've already taken my pills. I don't need anymore."

"That was this morning, Honey. These are for the afternoon."

Esther still refused.

"I'll see that she takes them," Justine volunteered. "She'll listen to me." She turned an innocent look on the nurse, knowing no one could talk Esther into anything she didn't want to do. Least of all her.

"Thank you." Mercy gave Esther's shoulder a gentle squeeze. "I just love this woman. She so sweet. She always have a smile for me."

Justine watched Mercy move to another table to administer drugs to another patient. As soon as the nurse was out of sight, Justine slipped the small cup of pills into her pocket and drank the water herself. Esther giggled, as if her big sister had just done her a favor.

Early the next morning Justine was back. Esther was already out on the balcony enjoying an already warm spring day. Mercy led her back into the visiting area where her sister was waiting for her at the corner table.

"Looks like you could use yourself a new manicure, Miss Justine," Mercy pointed out as she pushed Esther up to the table.

Justine clenched her hands in her lap, trying to hide her broken nails. Her hands were still red and raw from searching through the attic insulation, now her manicure was ruined, too. Pulling the bathroom wall down had been harder than she thought.

Mercy handed the paper cup of pills to Esther. "Will you be sure she takes these?" she asked Justine.

Justine nodded, but as soon as the nurse was out of earshot, she grabbed her sister by the wrist and took the cup of pills from her hand. "Where the hell is the money?"

Esther smiled sweetly at her. "What money?"

"I thought Father was coming yesterday. Didn't he tell you where his money was?"

"Don't be silly. Papa's been dead for twenty years. Have you lost your mind?"

Apparently so. Missing half her medications yesterday had not had the effect Justine was hoping for. Maybe missing the morning pills would.

Esther pushed herself away from the table. "I'm ready to go home now."

"I'm not taking you home. You're in a wheelchair. You can't walk."

"Mercy's coming with. She'll take care of me." Esther nodded primly. "I just want to sit down and play that old piano again. Remember when we used to hide there from Mama?"

"I sold the piano. It's expensive keeping up that old place and I was offered a good price."

"You didn't have to sell it. I told you where the money was—"

"It's not in the attic. And it's not behind the bathroom walls. There is no money, Esther." But there would be when Esther was dead and she sold that old place.

"Of course it's not." Esther wheeled herself toward the window, her slippered feet shuffling across the worn carpet. Justine stayed at the table. She didn't have to stand by the window to know what her sister was looking at.

Esther turned to look at Justine. "It's in the tree house."

Justine flinched. "Don't be ridiculous. Who'd ever hide money up there? What if the tree was hit by lightening –"

"It's still standing isn't it?"

Justine shuddered at the thought of climbing the tree. She'd never gone up in that tree house. Ever. There was no way she was going to attempt it at her age.

As if reading her thoughts, Esther said, "We could call Old Man Hawkins to go up there for us."

Justine snorted. Hawkins would charge for the service, tell them there was nothing up there and then steal the money for himself. Providing there was any money to steal.

"I helped Papa count it once," Esther said in a dreamy voice. "We used to sit up there planning where we'd go with all that money. Papa always wanted to go to Europe. I just wanted to go someplace warm."

Justine frowned. She remembered how jealous she had been every time her father and Esther would climb up that tree together. She wanted to follow, but couldn't. She also remembered Mother wanting to chop the whole thing down after Father had killed himself, but Esther had gotten hysterical and Mother had relented. She hadn't understood why Esther had been so upset. Now it all made sense. She was hiding all that money up there.

Justine stood at the base of the tree, trembling. She had given up trying to wrestle with the huge extension ladder by herself and had finally asked a neighbor boy to help her with it. When he had offered to go up and trim the tree for her, she had given him five bucks and told him to go to the movies. Now she regretted it.

The top of the ladder barely made it to the door of the little house nestled on the first branches of the old oak tree. The tree hadn't been this tall when she was a child. As the tree grew, the tree house towered even further from the ground than she remembered.

She clutched a rung of the ladder, the cold metal burning into her palm. She couldn't do this. Esther was crazy. There was no money up there. There couldn't be. She stretched her neck back looking up at the bottom of the small house their father had built for Esther. It was falling apart. There were holes in the floor and the squirrels had eaten a large hole next to the door. She'd probably find a nest of them inside. If she could only get up there.

The possibility of the money urged her on. White sand beaches and all she'd be able to do with that money flitted through her head. She remembered her father going up there to drink, to get away from her mother. Then, he had forbade Esther to go up there. By that time she and Esther were teenagers and were much more interested in stealing each other's boyfriends than in climbing trees. She hadn't put much weight in it back then, but now it all began to make sense. He didn't want them taking his money. That had to be it. He had been a cheap son-of-a-bitch, and he wanted it all to himself.

With a renewed courage and the promise of riches, she climbed up the ladder like a woman half her age. A woman who knew no fear. Taking in a deep breath, she reached for the handle of the tree house, almost giddy with the knowledge of what she would find there. The last thing she was expecting as she yanked open the old wooden door was the flock of angry black birds that flew into her face. She screamed, raising her arms to protect herself from the attacking crows. Her screams grew louder as the ladder tilted away from the tree and she rode it down to the ground with one final thud.

Esther set the binoculars in her lap, trying to hide a satisfied smile. "I guess I forgot to tell her about the crows."

"What crows would that be, dear?"

Esther shifted in her wheelchair, seeing an unfamiliar nurse standing behind her. "Where's Mercy?"

"Didn't she tell you? She handed in her resignation this morning."

Esther frowned and slowly turned away, raising the binoculars to her eyes again with a sense of dread. Mercy's old Ford was now parked in front of the house, its motor running. Justine's body still lay crumbled at the bottom of the ladder, but Mercy was now standing over her, wearing the suit she usually reserved for Sunday services. There were two beat-up looking suitcases at her feet.

"My money," Esther gasped, as Mercy turned in the direction of the nursing home and blew her a kiss before jumping into the car with the suitcases and driving away.

"What money?" the nurse asked her. "Did you lose something, darling?"

Esther almost choked on the words. "Mercy took my money."

The nurse unlocked the wheels of Esther's wheelchair and began pushing her back into the house. "Mercy would never take your money. Besides, she's half way to the airport by now. She said she was going somewhere warm."

Richard A. Thompson is a former civil engineer and building code official who traded his hardhat for a laptop and now writes full-time. He is the author of the Herman Jackson mysteries, about a Saint Paul bail bondsman with a shady past, and a stand-alone historical mystery, *Big Wheat*, which won the Minnesota Book Award. He has also published several short stories, one of which won the Boney Pete Award at Bloody Words in Toronto. He lives in Saint Paul with his wife, Caroline (since 1963,) a twenty-pound cat named Tank, and a slightly lighter one named Rags.

The Dark Under the Bed

Richard A. Thompson

They always come for you at night. In the dead still time after the cleaning crew has gone for the day and the nurse who comes on at eleven has made his rounds and settled in to dozing with his crossword puzzle, they come in twos or threes. When the morning deliverymen aren't due for several hours, nor the crew that cranks up the kitchen for the day, and it's so quiet you can hear the ballasts in the fluorescent lights out in the corridor, they come as silently as death itself. Sometimes there's just one. That's when it's the hardest to hear. They wear shoes with felt soles and tie up their trouser cuffs, like bicycle riders, so they make no sound of any kind. They kill quickly and silently.

If it's just one, he will leave the body where it lies. But if it's two or more, they will carry their victim out, leaving no trace. In the morning, even his bed sheets will be gone, and the orderlies will pretend the poor bastard never existed. The orderlies don't do the killing, but they're in on it. They all are.

I call them the shadow men. I have seen them.

Well, to be honest, I have seen their feet and legs. I sleep on the floor, under my bed, so they won't find me. But I have seen them pass by, so close I held my breath and clutched the souvenir samurai letter opener that I hide from the orderlies. It is my only protection at night. One night they went right past me and took old Ben Hicks, across the aisle. He fussed a little, but not for long. Then they carried him out, slung between them like an oversized sack of potatoes, the spots of their little mag lights picking out a path on the floor of the dark ward. I didn't like old Hicks much. He thought it was funny to fart in the chow line, and he read other people's mail when he could and stole things sometimes. Just little things, just to be an asshole. But he deserved better than that, I thought.

I've learned to keep quiet about it, of course. When I don't, people mostly think I'm either a liar or a crazy person, and I can hardly blame them. Maybe that's just as well. If the wrong people got the word that I know what's going on, I might suddenly get moved to the top of the list. I have absolutely no doubt that there is a list. And I am on it somewhere.

It came as a surprise, then, when somebody came along who wanted to talk about the shadow men.

It was at breakfast, a week or so after they had made Hicks disappear. I had made the mistake of sitting at a clean, empty table near a window. The mess hall at the old VA hospital has a nice view of the Mississippi River. If you get a table near the downstream end, you can even see the barges and tugs going through the locks at the Corps of Engineers dam, under the Ford Bridge. On both sides of the river, the early sun lights up the treetops above the bluffs and the Highland Park skyline looks golden. Used to be, you could maybe see some serious hotties through the breaks in the trees, too, jiggling in their shorts and halter-tops. Then they re-located the jogging trails on the west bank and ruined everything. Goddamn administration types would screw up a free lunch. Just like they did in the war.

Anyway, I was looking at the autumn colors, nymph-less though they were, and salting my imitation scrambled eggs when George Reagan put his tray down across from me. He's an ass-hole. He carries a radio around with him, and even though it has a plug for a headphone, he uses the speaker, loud, because it never occurs to him that the rest of the world doesn't share his taste in cornball music and dumbshit political commentary. He used to be a top kick in the infantry, and just because all the privates had to pretend to laugh at his bad jokes back then, he still thinks he must be somebody special. I wasn't in his goddamned infantry and have told him so several times. I've also told him he's not funny. I don't know why he hangs around me. If I'd noticed him sooner, I'd have picked a table full of dirty dishes. As far as I was concerned, he was an enemy infiltrator.

Where the hell did they come from? That ridge was empty a minute ago.

I don't know, but there's at least a dozen of them there now.

Take your SAW and light them up.

How do we know if they're hostile?

We ain't got the luxury of finding out. Light them up. Take the top of that damned ridge right off.

You got it.

"Well, Oddie, old buddy, we made it again, hey? The concrete mattresses tried to break our backs again but they couldn't do it. Hee, hee, hee." I swear to God, he giggles at his own stupid jokes just like an old woman.

"George, I'm not your buddy, and if you spout that tired old line one more time, my eggs are going to weep from boredom."

"That doesn't make any sense. How can eggs weep? Why are you wearing your pajama tops tucked into your pants, by the way? Old-timers disease catching up with you?"

"You're the fossil around here. This is a protest."

"What's it protesting, shirts? Hee, hee, hee."

Why the hell don't the shadow men take him? I'd gladly hold the flashlight for them.

"The orderlies gave me hell for sleeping on the floor again," I said. "This is to let them know that any rule that isn't in writing, I don't have to pay any attention to."

"You know, that's another thing that doesn't make—"

"Wow, there's a full tank top." I pretended to be peering around him, looking out the window. "And her legs go all the way up to her ass, too."

"Really? Where?"

He turned around in his chair and craned his neck, and I reached across the table and dumped his glass of orange juice onto his lap.

"Hey! Those were clean ODs today!"

"Clumsy bastard."

"You saying I did that myself? You're crazy. Everybody says so."

"Everybody is right." I grabbed his radio and threw it across the room. It hit the tile floor, bounced a few times, and went quiet. "If I were you, I'd stay away from me."

"Jesus, you really are crabby today. I'm going to go sit some-place else."

"And they say infantrymen are stupid." I allowed myself a little smile and some extra pepper on my eggs.

"That was pretty slick. Are you the one they call Odds?" I hadn't heard the new speaker come up and sit beside me. That bothered me, since I work at being hard to surprise.

You let one of them get away. Next time I tell you to light somebody up—

Yeah, yeah.

Now we've got to kill him at close quarters.

Then we will, okay?

I turned and looked the guy over. I hadn't seen him before. He wasn't old enough to be either Korea or 'Nam, and he didn't look fucked up enough to be here just for injuries. He had a USMC tattoo on his right bicep, and he was wearing cammi cargo pants and a white tee shirt. He didn't wear a silly-ass grin or call me his buddy, so I gave him a curt nod and left his orange juice alone.

"Who told you my name?"

"Some guy who said I shouldn't sit here."

"He was probably right."

"Is that really your name, or was he being a smartass?"

"It's short for Odysseus. But people like Odds or Oddie because it sounds like I'm some kind of screwed-up antisocial type."

"Are you?"

"Yes."

"Afghanistan?"

"Korengal Valley," I said, nodding.

"Hard ground. I was with Tenth Mountain Division. Ran an M40A1. They call me Sid."

He was a sniper, was what he had just told me. That could explain why he was a patient, even though he looked fit enough. Snipers get a lot of head problems. We didn't say anything stupid like, "semper fi," but we shook hands. I turned back to my imitation eggs.

"They say you've seen them," said my new acquaintance.

"Who?"

"Who says, or who have you seen?"

"Don't be cute."

"Okay, I won't," he said. "The night people. The ones who make people disappear."

"Somebody's putting you on," I said.

"Yeah, and his name is Odysseus. I've seen them, too, is the thing. And nobody believes me, either. What do you think it means?"

"Means? It means that we're somebody's bad conscience. We weren't supposed to come back if we weren't whole, is the thing. But we weren't smart enough to figure that out, so somebody has to correct our mistake."

"Yeah, but what about Hicks, say? He wasn't our war, he was Korea. Why would they pick him?"

"Maybe they make mistakes. Maybe he pissed them off. Why ask me?"

"Because I think somebody ought to do something about it, and I think you do, too."

"Oh really? Like what?" I had no idea if I could trust him, but he definitely had my attention.

"Kill a few. Then maybe the others aren't so eager to come back. Isn't that how you win any war?"

"I couldn't say," I said. "I was never in any that we won. You know, I think these eggs are rancid. I'll see you around, okay?" I got up, took my tray, and left him there.

That night they came for Bates. They were upping the pace.

Three of them, over by the wall. See?

No, my damn night goggles need new batteries.

Then hunt by Braille. Get out your K-bar.

I think they've gone already. Damn, they are fast.

They'll be back. Next time, we give them a souvenir. You can do that, can't you?

Worry about yourself, not me.

The next day I found Sid playing ping-pong with a guy in a wheelchair. His name was Sanchez, and he'd been around for about a year. Shortly after they started teaching him about using the chair, he put a homemade bomb under it. He was pissed because the guys who had actually lost their legs got artificial ones, while he never would. But he didn't use a big enough charge, and all he managed to do was burn himself on the backs of his legs and his ass. I guess nobody had explained to him that you couldn't blow your ass off and get a new one. He was one bitter son of a bitch, but he was a good ping-pong player. The only guaranteed putaway shot that Sid had was to make the ball bounce so high that Sanchez couldn't reach it, and he didn't get a chance to do that very often.

I stood off to the side, pretending to be a net judge, and Sid kept playing while he talked to me out of the side of his mouth.

"Are you ready to do something?" he said.

"Maybe. You want to go someplace and talk?"

"You can talk in front of Sanchez. He doesn't want in, but he won't rat us out, either."

"Anybody will rat you out, man. Anybody. What the hell, we even had a president who did."

"Fair enough. Meet me in the smoker in an hour."

"Done," I said. As I walked away, I dimly heard somebody behind me say, "Crazy fucker, now he even talks to people who aren't there." I didn't know whom they were talking about.

This is a high-risk operation. I don't want anything but volunteers.

Do we have a choice?

No.

Then I'm in.

Just remember, you volunteered.

We got cold Cokes for fifty cents from a machine that was supposed to be subsidized by the DAV. I didn't know if that was true or not, but it made a nice story.

"Do we have something that looks like a plan?" I said.

"Just like in the mountains, man. We patrol the known trails. If they see us first, we get the hell out, no hesitation, no exceptions. But if we see them first, we take them out from behind, fast and silent. Leave nobody alive."

"When?"

"Tonight."

"I have no weapon."

"I can get you a K-bar."

"Then I'm in."

"Double-oh thirty, by the west water cooler. Don't bring anything that makes noise."

"Yeah, I heard that somewhere once. See you there."

The rest of the day was very, very long. I watched a bunch of soap operas in the day room, because they are so goddamned boring. In front of them, I could sleep standing up. Later I got a book from the library and read a couple of chapters. I have no idea what it was about. I walked around the grounds a bunch.

Suit up now, people, and sleep with your gear. I'll wake you up half an hour early so you can have a shot of coffee with gunpowder in it, get good and hot. Figure on getting bloody tonight. If you also get back, that's a bonus.

I was at the cooler exactly on time. I could tell Sid liked that. He gave me a tight hint of a smile as he handed me the weapon. We said nothing. Hell, we didn't even *breathe* loud. I pointed two fingers at my eyes and he shook his head no, telling me he hadn't seen anybody.

We were at the part of the corridor system farthest from the sleeping rooms. We took opposite sides of the corridor and worked our way inward, silently darting from doorway to doorway. I could hear my pulse roaring in my ears.

We don't use string anymore, but there's a link between you and your partner. A solid link, even though it's just air. Anybody gets in that space, you should know it immediately and be ready to kill immediately. There ain't no innocent bystanders here. Odds?

Gunny?

You ready to kick some?

I'm ready to do more than that, Gunny.

All right, then. Move out.

I loosened my grip on the knife and tightened it up again, just to stay familiar with the bulk of it. It was a good weapon, heavy and sharp. My arm longed to slash with it.

There.

At the collection area of two squad bays, a figure in black, moving fast.

You think he saw us?

Doesn't matter. There's only one. Take him out.

The lights were out in the squad bay, and we waited a moment for our eyes to adjust.

You see anything?

I told you before, my goggles don't work.

Check the racks. Maybe he's pretending to be a patient.

There, there, there! He's in Reagan's rack. I've got him, Sid.

What the hell are you doing?

There's something wrong with my knife. It's flimsy, like. I've got to strangle him.

No, man, he's one of ours!

No way, Gunny.

Odds, get off.

Go straight to hell.

Move in now, people! Get him off, get him off! Cuff him. Tase him if you have to.

Total melee. Shadow men everywhere. The fight spilling out into the corridor. A blinding pain in the back of my neck. Then total blackness.

*

I'm not sure how many we took out, but they gave me a commendation for the night patrol, and a promotion. They still misspell the abbreviation for my rank, but now it has an unmistakable "Advanced" in front of it, which is nice.

I have a new room now, which is also nice. It's a private room, and they even gave me a lock for the door, so I don't have to sleep on the floor all the time. Some people say the lock is phony, but nobody has come in while I had it locked, so I'm satisfied that it works. They say the killings have stopped now, but I don't believe it. They're still in the building, and there's still a list. But I think they're afraid of me now. They don't come for me, even though my new room has a neat little plastic name plaque on the door. It says:

Boosalis, Odysseus G.

Advanced PTSD

I don't know what became of Sid. I think the shadow men must have gotten him.

They say we have waffles for breakfast today. Life is good.

Michael Allan Mallory writes the Snake Jones zoo mystery series with Marilyn Victor. *Death Roll* (2007), their debut novel, introduced mystery's first zoologist sleuth with "...engaging characters and an intriguing behind-the-scenes look at zoo life." (Kirkus Reviews). In *Killer Instinct* (2011), zookeeper Lavender "Snake" Jones returned to investigate a wild wolf killing in the North Woods of Minnesota that escalates into the murder of a key suspect. Michael's volunteer jags at the International Wolf Center in Ely, Minnesota, provided much of the background for the story. CrimeSpree Magazine called *Killer Instinct* "both a great entertainment and a compelling mystery, with a strong sense of place... and really cool, interesting characters."

Michael's short stories have appeared in numerous anthologies, most notably *Resort to Murder*, *Deadly Treats*, and *Writes of Spring*. Michael is a member of Mystery Writers of America, and is a past president of the Twin Cities chapter of Sisters in Crime. His writing has appeared in *Mystery Scene Magazine* and *Mystery Readers Journal*. He lives in St. Louis Park with his delightful wife and two lively cats. His website is **www.snakejones.com.**

Desperados

Michael Allan Mallory

The getaway car was dead. Like ready for the junkyard dead. Sappo cranked the starter one more time. The engine coughed once before it wheezed into heart breaking silence.

"Shit!" Sappo pounded the steering wheel. "Shit! Shit! Shit!" He'd had a potty mouth ever since I first met him in grade school. In those days he was Joey Sapporella. Still is, come to think of it. I'm just used to calling him Sappo. He turned to me with a face jackhammered off a rock quarry. He'd always been spooky looking, with cruel eyes and dark angry eyebrows ready to jump off his forehead at you.

"What?" I asked. He was throwing off a weird vibe.

"This is your fault, Dwayne."

"My fault? How's this my fault?"

"You stole a shitty car."

"How was I supposed to know the freakin' car would die five minutes into our getaway?"

His mouth formed a hard line but he said nothing. Sappo knew I was right, he just couldn't admit it.

I shrugged. "So what're we gonna do?"

"Ditch the car—"

Police sirens screamed dangerously close. We both jerked upright, glancing this way and that along the quiet residential street. One and half story homes, green lawns, tall boulevard trees, but no cops.

A big exhale. I'd forgotten to breathe. "That was close."

"Yeah, like two blocks away."

"And quick."

Another siren from the opposite direction.

"Geez!" I nearly jumped out of my skin.

"They must be sending in cops from all over."

"The guard, Sappo, you shouldn't've killed the bank guard."

"Hey, the dumbass had to play hero. I told him to hit the floor but he didn't listen. Just shows you can't trust nobody."

"But you killed him, man!"

"Better him than us." Which was Sappo's philosophy in a nutshell. He angled his head to give me one of his you're-a-moron looks. "Didn't think of that, did you? For a guy with such a big head, you'd think there'd be something in there to fill it." Sappo didn't take criticism well but, boy, he sure enjoyed dishing it out. It didn't bother me. I was used to him. Others weren't so forgiving, which is why he didn't have many friends—many old friends. Sooner or later, if you hung around him long enough, he'd find some way to slam you.

Halfway out of the car, Sappo said, "Grab the money."

Oh, I wasn't going to leave that behind! I reached into the rear seat and hoisted the bulky black sports bag up and out. The heft was satisfying. Bricks and bricks of sweet cash.

We abandoned our ride, rushed to the curb and up the lawn of the nearest house. A last glance at the white sedan didn't give me warm fuzzies. The car screamed it was abandoned. The only thing we had going was it was early afternoon on a work day in the suburbs, so not many pedestrians to see us hotfoot it. We hurried between the two houses into the alley where we slowed to a hurried walk. Cutting over two more blocks to Kentucky Avenue, we ducked down another alley, hoping we'd put enough distance between us and the car.

"Slow down, Dwayne. Try to blend in."

Easy for him to say. Sappo didn't exactly blend in either. Black sweatshirt, dark jeans, short black hair and stubby beard, he looked like a refugee from a drug bust. Even in his baby pictures he looks like a hardened criminal. "Crazy Eyes" some poor schmuck had called him once in gym class. Bad move. Sappo stuffed the kid's face with a knuckle sandwich. It earned him detention but Sappo didn't care. Standing up for himself was what mattered.

"Where we going?" I didn't like being in the open with so many cops around.

"Gotta find a place to hole up. Get off the street."

"I'm with you there. How 'bout that yellow house?"

We'd just walked by a newly remodeled home with green shutters and a hot tub on a new cedar deck. Sappo no likey. "Too ritzy. Owners with attitude. Bet it has an alarm system. No, that one." He gazed in the direction of a tidy bungalow with blue Dutch lap siding and white awnings. Between the house and detached garage ran a curving flower garden of bright colors tended to by a woman in a denim skirt, tea-colored blouse, straw hat and sandals. She misted a row of purple pansies with a garden sprayer. Behind her—Sappo pointed out—the rear door of the house yawned open like an invitation.

Putting on his best face and manners, Sappo crossed the driveway. I hung back so the lady wouldn't feel intimidated. Sappo says I come across like a wounded musk ox.

Sappo cleared his throat. "Sorry to bother you, ma'am. Our car broke down a few blocks over. We need a tow. Can we use your phone?"

The woman offered a friendly smile, one full of grace that made her seem younger than she was. She was old, like maybe fifty. Pushing up the straw hat, she gave us the once-over. "I thought all young people had cell phones these days."

"We do, in our trunk. We locked the keys inside."

"I hate when that happens. Isn't that frustrating?"

"Sure is. Um, can we use your phone?"

"Oh, of course. It's in the kitchen. A lot of people no longer have land lines but we do. This way." Setting down the garden sprayer, the woman led us over stone pavers to the rear door. Once inside the kitchen she motioned to a retro AT&T Trimline hanging on the wall by the window.

Sappo closed the door behind him and locked it. When he turned around the smile was wiped from his face. "I lied. We're not here for the phone." From beneath his sweatshirt he pulled out a Ruger pistol tucked in his belt. The old woman flinched. "That's right," Sappo went on, "we're armed and dangerous. Do what we tell you and you won't get hurt."

Panic flashed across her face before she managed to regain her composure. The woman wasn't going to give in that easily. She sized us up again with a critical eye, the way my grandmother used to after I tracked in mud on her clean carpet. The creases by her eyes deepened as she focused on the black bag under my arm. "What did you do, rob a bank?"

"That's pretty good," I said, impressed. "It was Citizens Federated at Knollwood."

"*Dwayne*," Sappo shot me a warning glance. Then to the woman. "What's your name?"

"Alice. Alice Chatsky."

"Who else is here, Alice?"

"Just me and Oliver, my husband."

"Where is he?"

"The front yard."

Sappo nodded to me. "Find him."

Turned out I didn't have to. He found us. The sound of the front door opening and closing was followed by footsteps from the living room. "Something's going on, Alice. Something big. Two police cars just drove by with flashing lights."

Sappo and I locked eyes.

The voice got closer. "Must be an accident. Wouldn't surprise me with all the construction on Highway 7. Didn't see—" Around the corner appeared a stocky white haired man with tortoise shell glasses. His plaid shirt had a button missing over a well stocked beer belly. "Alice, who are these men?" Guess he'd figured out we weren't the Publishers Clearing House Prize Patrol dudes with a big check.

Alice removed her straw hat and set it on the counter next to a glass vase of happy daisies. She smoothed down her brownish grey hair. "These are the men the police are looking for."

Oliver Chatsky's eyes got big. They got bigger when Sappo stepped over with the Ruger. "She's right. I already killed one fool today. Don't give me a reason to kill another."

Oliver nodded.

"Give us your car keys and we'll go."

The old couple looked at each other awkwardly.

"*What?*"

In a timid voice, Oliver said, "We don't have a car. We loaned it to our daughter. Hers is in the shop."

"No car?" Sappo deflated like a punctured tire. We just couldn't catch a break today. I set down the sports bag on the black and white tiled floor. It felt heavy all of a sudden.

"Now we're stuck here," Sappo groaned.

Oliver's face filled with concern. "Stuck here? No, you have to leave. Our daughter's coming at six with the kids."

That got Sappo's motor running. "Your daughter? With the car?"

The old man's face went pale. He'd said the wrong thing and knew it. "No, you have to be gone by then."

"*Shut up!*" Sappo violently whipped out his arm. The gun butt smashed into the flower vase, which exploded into a spray of glass, water, and daisies. "*I can do any fucking thing I want! You got that?*"

The Chatsky's stared back in shock. Sappo's a mean looking son of a bitch when he's angry. Remember Crazy Eyes?

"You win," Oliver murmured in a beaten voice.

Sappo grunted with satisfaction. It was all about proving who was top dog.

Surveying the destruction around her, Alice sighed. "Can I clean up this mess now?"

Not long after that we moved to the living room where nobody talked. It was like being at a funeral for a relative you never knew. No one had anything to say and just waited for the thing to end. Alice and Oliver sat next to each other on a brown sofa, holding hands and watching us anxiously. I was in a padded chair while Sappo hovered by the picture window, off to side so he couldn't be seen from the street.

"Hold on." He leaned closer to the glass. "Mailman's coming."

I joined him by the curtain. The mailman had crossed the street and was going from house to house. In the window I caught the Chatsky's reflection. They looked scared and I felt bad for them. They reminded me of my grandparents and it bothered me we were putting them through this ordeal.

The metallic clank of the mailbox pulled my attention outside. Sappo's breathing grew heavier and his right hand clenched. He scowled at the outside wall as if he could see through it. Only after the mailman moved on to the neighbors did Sappo finally relax.

"Excuse me."

It was Oliver. He'd been pretty antsy for the last minute, shifting his weight on the sofa cushion like he had a bug up his butt. Finally he cleared his throat. "There's something you should to know."

That didn't sound good.

"You don't want trouble," Oliver went on. "We don't want trouble. But you have to let me outside to mow the grass."

"No fucking way I'm letting you outside."

"Then that could be a problem."

Sappo leveled one of his you-must-be-a-moron looks.

"I'm serious." Oliver didn't back down. "Our lawn mower died a few days ago. I borrowed one from the guy across the street. The house with the asphalt driveway. That's Walt's place."

"So?"

"I cut my grass every three weeks. With all the rain last week, you can see it needs it. I was about to start when you guys showed up."

"And why do I care?"

Oliver pushed his glasses up and spoke the next words carefully. "My neighbors know my routine. If I leave the lawn uncut another week they'll think something's wrong. I borrowed Walt's mower to get it done today. The thing is he wants me to return it by three. If I don't get the mower to him by then he'll come for it. You don't want that."

Sappo shrugged. "Maybe he won't come."

"Oh, he will," Alice jumped in. "Walt is nosey."

"Very nosey." Oliver said.

"Fine, take the mower back now."

"Without cutting the grass? He'd ask questions."

"Just leave it in his front yard and walk away."

"He'd call," Oliver explained. "Listen, I'm just trying to avoid trouble. If I don't cut the grass and return the mower in that order, Walt will be a pest."

Alice nodded in agreement.

For a while Sappo said nothing, he just shook his head. "What d'you think, Dwayne?"

Me? He wanted my opinion? That didn't happen every day. But he wasn't kidding so I gave the matter serious thought. "This

Walt dude sounds like a pain in the butt. Maybe cutting the grass is the way to go."

Sappo's dark eyes burned a hole in the carpet as he weighed his options. "I don't like it...but I don't want that chump over here asking questions. Okay, cut the grass." He glared a warning at Oliver. "*That's all*. Don't talk to nobody."

"I won't."

"Not even your best friend."

"I understand."

"And don't take all day."

Oliver rose from the sofa with Alice still clutching his hand, gazing into his eyes meaningfully. With a troubled smile, he gently released her hand. At the front door he eased onto a small bench where he bent forward with a grunt to lace up an old pair of Chuck Taylor sneakers.

Sappo hovered above him, arms folded across his chest. "Don't screw up."

Oliver swallowed hard, nodded and stepped out the front door.

"Watch him, Dwayne," Sappo said. "Make sure he doesn't do anything stupid."

A two stroke engine roared to life. Oliver pushed the lawn mower across the front yard, leaving a clear cut path behind him. He kept his head down and stuck to business. The front yard sloped down at a steep angle to the sidewalk where it was more difficult to maneuver. He changed directions often, cutting in and out over the green fringe in no easy pattern. He was never out of sight, not for one moment. Even at the bottom of the slope we could still see him from the shoulders up. Every so often he'd glance at the big front window. Maybe to make sure we were still watching, maybe to convince himself we weren't about to go ballistic on him. Or Alice. Whatever the reason, he moved pretty darn fast for an old guy with a gut.

"Not the best mow job I've ever seen." I craned my neck to see. "He's leaving some ragged spots."

"What do you expect?" Alice fired back, eyes burning. "He's going as fast as he can so he can return the mower. And you're criticizing him for not doing a perfect job!"

I turned away, ashamed. Normally I don't irritate nice old

ladies. Sappo didn't care, he wasn't paying attention. He was distracted by something outside.

"Just a sec—"

A female runner was coming up the sidewalk in a U of M T-shirt and maroon shorts. Her pony tail swished from side to side with each step. The closer she got the more anxious Sappo got. But Oliver ignored her. He kept his eyes down and pushed the mower without so much as a glance her way.

"Good boy," Sappo snorted from the edge of the window as she disappeared out of view.

The old man quickly finished the side and backyard. Killing the engine, he wheeled the silent red Toro across the street and up the blacktop of Walt's driveway. He parked the mower by the front steps, rang the doorbell, turned and started back. Walt appeared on his front stoop. Middle-aged. Hawaiian shirt. Cargo shorts. Hairy legs. He glanced down at the mower, to Oliver, who was at the curb by now, then stared across the street at the Chatskey's house and front yard with confusion. Not the brightest bulb, I guess. Finally, Walt pushed the mower to his garage.

"You didn't screw up." Sappo locked the front door behind Oliver.

"Now what happens?"

"We wait."

And we did. An hour, maybe two. Time dragged on with the four of us in the Chatsky's living room. Sappo had switched on a radio so he could hear if there was any breaking news about the bank robbery. By now my stomach was not a happy camper. We hadn't eaten all day and after some false starts my belly finally decided to let people know about it, loudly. All heads turned toward me.

I shrugged. "I'm hungry."

Sappo motioned to the lady of the house. "Make us something."

Alice Chatsky, who'd been adjusting a red lacquered music box, smacked it down on the side table. "Let me understand. You takeover our house, hold us prisoner, and now you expect us to feed you?"

Sappo stared her down. "Yeah, I do."

A hardness came over her face like she could chew railroad spikes. She looked for guidance from Oliver, who shook his head as if to say: don't make trouble. Alice's narrow shoulders slowly unbunched. "Fine," she grumbled and started for the kitchen. "Don't expect much, just sandwiches."

"I'm coming with you." Sappo followed in her footsteps, jerking his head toward Oliver. "Keep an eye on him."

A minute went by. Oliver sucked in deep breaths like he was summoning up his courage. Finally, after a glance toward the kitchen, he wandered over by me. "You seem like a decent man," he said. "Your friend, though, he's on the edge. It won't take much to push him over."

I knew that. Shooting that bank guard bothered me. Sappo could be violent but he'd never killed anyone before.

"The longer the two of you stay the more dangerous it gets for you."

I shook my head. "Too many cops out there right now. Anyway, Sappo won't go for it."

"He might listen to you."

The poor sap didn't know who he was dealing with. "Let me tell you about Sappo, when he gets like this he won't listen to anybod—"

RING…RING…

The phone.

My heart seized up. You forget how loud those old fashioned wall phones can be.

"Don't answer that!" Sappo ordered from the kitchen. A second later he rushed into the living room to make sure Oliver hadn't gotten the other extension. "Don't answer. That might be your neighbor."

After the last ring died, Sappo ran a hand through his hair and released the breath he'd been holding, as if he'd just dodged a bullet. He returned to the kitchen where not more than two minutes later his voice exploded.

"*You bitch!*"

Oliver's head snapped toward the sound and he was off like a rocket. I ran after him. In the kitchen we found Alice jammed against the refrigerator with Sappo looming over her like a rabid hyena, hand raised and ready to strike. "She unlocked the door, Dwyane! Unlocked the fucking door!" His hand came down. Alice turned away—eyes jammed tight—to receive the blow. It never landed. Oliver jumped in to block it.

"You don't touch her!"

Sappo, startled by the old man's defiance, recovered and sucker punched him in his big gut. Oliver doubled over with a grimace. Yanking out the pistol, Sappo rasped, "*Enough of this shit.* You're dead, asshole."

"No—" Alice choked with horror.

I stepped in and grabbed Sappo's arm.

"Dwayne, what the fuck are you doing?"

My fingers tightened like a clamp. "No more shooting."

"*Dwayne.*"

He glared at me but I didn't let go.

RING…RING…

"Don't answer!" Sappo jerked his arm free and lowered the gun.

The phone rang out.

And that's when I noticed it. On Sappo. A tiny red dot on his chest. Before I could say anything there was a loud crash from the window, flying glass and a loud bang that scared the crap out of me. The kitchen door exploded open and three cops in black SWAT vests, helmets and big ass guns stormed in.

"Police! Drop the weapon!"

More SWAT cops. "On the floor! Show us your hands!"

Next thing I knew I was kissing the vinyl floor with an elbow in my back and getting flexcuffed. Near my face I saw a flashbang stick. Like a big fire cracker, it had made the loud bang.

I don't remember much after that. It was a blur of black duty boots, semi-automatic weapons and shoving. Sappo and I were pulled to our feet while a SWAT cop spoke to the Chatsky's. Turns out it was a SWAT negotiator on the phone earlier trying to contain the situation. When no one answered, the cops decided to storm in to take Sappo before he got a chance to kill Oliver.

How the hell did they know where we were?

For the life of me, I couldn't figure it out. Far as I knew, no one had seen us slip in through the backyard.

Eventually we were taken out the front door. Cops were everywhere. In the neighbors' yard. On the street. A St. Louis Park squad car pulled up to the curb and the rear doors opened for us. Sappo didn't talk, he was too pissed off. It wasn't until we got to the sidewalk that I saw it, wasn't until after they put us in the back of the prowler that I realized what I was seeing. Cut into the grass on the sloping front yard of the Chatsky's house were the words: HELP. CALL 911.

Sneaky, Oliver, very sneaky. And gutsy. I didn't think you had it in you. Across the street, Walt stood on his front stoop grinning like fool. As the cops closed the doors on us, I decided Sappo was right: you can't trust nobody.

Jess Lourey is the author of the Lefty-nominated Murder-by-Month mysteries set in Battle Lake, Minnesota, featuring amateur sleuth Mira James and her sidekick Mrs. Berns. *Booklist* gave her latest, *November Hunt*, a starred review, writing, "It's not easy to make people laugh while they're on the edge of their seats, but Lourey pulls it off!" Jess has been teaching writing and sociology at the college level since 1998.

When not raising her wonderful kids, teaching, or writing, you can find her gardening, traveling, and navigating the niceties and meanities of small-town life. She is a member of Sisters in Crime, The Loft, and serves on the national board of Mystery Writers of America

Death By Potato Salad

Jess Lourey

Mrs. Berns' form-fitting, black t-shirt read "80 is the new 30." She wore elastic-waisted pants, not because she was large but because at her age, every second counted. She was, in fact, a trim woman whose hair was currently the color of an overripe apricot, who couldn't see past her nose without her thick-rimmed cat eye glasses, and who didn't stay in the lines when she colored and so certainly wasn't going to bother when she applied lipstick. She'd lived long enough to recognize that life was always good, even when it was bad. This is why she had a slight twinkle in her eye as she kneeled next to the corpse in the bright light of the kitchen and uttered these three grim words:

"Clearly, it's murder."

May in Battle Lake is a beautiful time of the year. The new green of the leaves convinces people that maybe winter wasn't really that bad, and the lilac blossoms perfume the air with a sweet purple honey. Why Mrs. Berns had allowed Pastor Winter to talk her into leaving all this beauty to head north to Bemidji, Minnesota, for the All Church weekend retreat was anyone's guess. Well, really, it was her guess: she wanted a little action, and she'd already run through all the decent prospects in Battle Lake. With the motto, "You're never too late for a coed slumber party" in the forefront of her mind, she'd boarded the orange school bus and headed upstate toward the land of Paul Bunyan.

The All Church weekend retreat had begun ten years ago, the idea being to bring together church-going Minnesotans of all denominations to celebrate faith and forge common ground. It being Minnesota, the retreat drew Presbyterians, Catholics, and Lutherans. Mrs. Berns could pick out a Presbyterian at 100 feet by the way the ladies clutched their purses. The Catholics were harder to identify as they went to great lengths, she thought, to blend in, but more often than not, they couldn't leave the house without a cross around their neck and an apology on their lips, so they were easy to spot if you got close enough. The Lutherans, well, they were her people.

The retreat had been held at the Morningwood Lodge since its inception, based on the theory that Bemidji is equally far away from everyone. The Lodge was actually three sprawling buildings, each named for a northern Minnesota animal, spread over 30 acres of lakeside property. Because over 120 people had registered for the retreat this year, it was held in the Moose building, the largest. Upon entering the Moose, all participants were assigned rooms and asked to return to the main hall as soon as they'd unpacked.

The first thing Mrs. Berns had noticed after dropping off her bags and upon entering the main hall was that the gender ratio was 70/30 women to men, an imbalance she'd grown accustomed to in the last decade or so. It turns out that life is a race won by women, a fact that gives her the giggles every time she thinks about it. The second thing she noticed was a very tall gentleman clad in pleated khakis and a white polo shirt that accented his beautifully wrinkled, tan skin. He must have recently returned from the south, another point in his favor. What really hooked her, though, was the thick white mustache that hung on each side of his mouth like a welcome mat. She was a sucker for facial hair. His name tag read "Joe," and he was standing on the edge of the crowd rather than taking a seat. Mrs. Berns didn't usually date in her age group, but when in Rome.

She threaded her way through the throng and nudged him in the side. "Come here often?"

He turned to her, startled. "No. This is my second time."

Mrs. Berns pursed her lips and tried again. "With a great mustache comes great responsibility." She winked so he couldn't possibly miss the innuendo this time, but rather than smile back, he blushed and glanced around the packed main hall with immense interest, as if the hundred-odd geriatrics milling about had suddenly begun krumping. Had Mrs. Berns pegged him wrong? Was he really an old man, rather than a good time with wrinkles? Before she could shoot her last rocket and ask him what a girl did around here for fun, the crowd began to move with intention.

"What's happening?" she asked.

He pointed at the white screen at the head of the main hall. It read, "Day One Icebreaker Classes" in a holy font. Underneath were five selections:

- Advanced Hotdish
- Miracles with Mayonnaise
- How to See God in the Face of Your Enemies (Church Committee Mediation Techniques)
- Christian Crafts
- The Art of Funeral Small Talk

The All Church director, a man named William with a ready smile and a silver mane of hair, was grouping attendees according to where they wanted to spend the afternoon. Not yet ready to give up on the whiff of excitement she'd felt when she'd first set eyes on Joe, Mrs. Berns tailed him to a group, and then followed that group into a classroom. It wasn't until she was inside that she realized she'd chosen "Miracles of Mayonnaise."

In the front of the kitchen classroom, a white-haired woman grinned widely at them. She had a whiteboard behind her and eggs, lemon, vinegar, mustard, salt, and canola oil on the table in front of her. The room housed eight other stations, each of them consisting of a table holding up the same ingredients.

"Welcome," the teacher said, clasping her hands together. "You have now entered the wonderful world of mayonnaise. My name is Mrs. Zindahl, and I'll be guiding you on your journey today. Before we begin, however, I must issue a warning. Homemade mayonnaise is the pufferfish of the church kitchen, deadly if not prepared properly. But mmmm is it delicious when you do it right!"

Mrs. Berns grimaced and studied her competition, Mrs. Zindahl, continuing to gush about mayo in the background. Joe stood across the room with two other men, one who resembled a dumpling and the other a green bean that'd been in the microwave too long. Two single women besides her and the teacher had also taken the class. One of those women was making googly eyes at Joe. The room also held three married couples, two of them standing near

Mrs. Berns and the other leaning against the industrial refrigerator in the back of the room. The refrigerator couple appeared very much in love, probably a second marriage. The husband seemed to be in his 80s, but the wife was young, no more than 70. Of the two couples standing next to her, one was unremarkable, and the other gave her the willies. The husband had been making fun of his wife since they'd walked in. She'd kept trying to laugh off what he said, but her eyes seemed both tired and sad.

"I don't even know why we walked into this class," he was saying, his voice low enough not to interrupt the teacher but loud enough that everyone within five feet could hear him, "when you're already a g-d scientist in the kitchen. We should have gone to funeral small talk so you could learn something about making conversation."

It was his fourth put-down in as many minutes. The wife seemed to shrink into herself. The other couple inched away imperceptibly. Mrs. Berns tapped him on the shoulder. "Excuse me."

The husband turned, an expectant smile on his face. "Yah?"

"Did you just say 'g-d' instead of 'goddamn?'"

He winked at her. "It *is* a church retreat."

"You're an asshole." Mrs. Berns strolled to the back of the room and ended up standing near the second-marriage couple, whom, she noticed, were taking great pains to avoid looking at the obnoxious husband whose side she had just left. That's when William, the retreat's director, entered, a brilliant smile on his face. He swept the room with it, but the grin faltered when he laid eyes on the rude man. Mrs. Berns guessed it wasn't the awful husband's first time at the retreat.

"Am I too late to join the fun?" William asked, planting his smile back on his face.

"You're perfectly on time," Mrs. Zindahl said. "I was just about to break everyone into pairs. Please all, locate a partner and then choose a cooking station."

Mrs. Berns made a beeline toward Joe, but the other woman who'd been googly-eying him was quicker. Mrs. Berns had let the woman's walker fool her, but she wouldn't make that mistake twice.

"Do you have a partner?"

Mrs. Berns turned to the doughy woman who'd appeared at her side. The woman's hair was shockingly brown against her wrinkled features. Mrs. Berns didn't trust the lady, both because as a whitehair she could dye her do any color she chose and had gone with boring brown, and because the woman hadn't once glanced at Joe. But what choice did Mrs. Berns have? She shrugged. "No, but you better not slow me down."

As they made their way to a station, the woman introduced herself by tapping on her name tag. "I'm Tabitha. My friends call me Tabby."

Mrs. Berns held out her hand. "Mrs. Berns."

Tabby nodded across the room at the obnoxious husband and his meek wife. "That's Hiram and Lucille. They come every year."

"Is he always so rude?"

Tabby's eyes widened, and then she dropped them, a blush creeping up her cheeks. She changed the subject rather than answer. "This is the perfect class for me. I just started the Norwegian diet last week. I can only eat white food. I haven't lost any weight yet, but it's early."

Mrs. Berns made a point of not talking as they mixed the ingredients, which was no problem as Tabby chattered enough for the both of them. First, Mrs. Berns separated an egg and stirred together the yolk, lemon juice, vinegar, mustard, and 1/2 teaspoon salt until it turned bright yellow. Like most women of her generation, she'd been cooking since the time she could walk. Although she had her favorites, she didn't mind learning a new recipe now and again. The main ingredients blended, Mrs. Berns whisked while Tabby drizzled in ¾ of a cup of canola oil into the main mixture, one drop at a time, until they had a thick, fluffy bowl of mayonnaise. Mrs. Berns was sweating but proud of the final product. The only factor taking the edge off of her joy was Hiram's continual criticism of Lucille two stations over. Mrs. Berns wanted to bop him on the head and vowed to do just that next time he came close.

Once everyone's mayonnaise was complete, Mrs. Zindahl gave each station the opportunity to select one dish from the All Church cookbook to create with their fresh mayonnaise. Mrs. Berns selected tuna salad without consulting Tabby, who, to be fair, had done little so far. They were directed to retrieve the necessary ingredients from the refrigerator and the pantry in the back of the room. Mrs. Berns tried to catch Joe's eye when she went for the onions and he for the garlic, but he seemed to be avoiding her glance. She shrugged. His loss.

Twenty minutes later, Mrs. Zindahl declared it time to pass the dishes around for a mayo bliss taste test. Everyone was given a set of tasting spoons, and the big glass bowls traveled from station to station. Mrs. Berns decided to use the same spoon each time, figuring it'd save on dishes later. The concoctions ranged from disgusting—the mayonnaise snickers marshmallow delight—to heavenly—Lucille's potato salad. The salad was creamy, not too heavy on the dressing, with the perfect amount of celery crunch and tangy salt. Hiram had been right about his wife. She really knew what she was doing in the kitchen. A person wouldn't know it by him, though. Because his wife had passed their dish to her left at Mrs. Zindahl's request, Hiram was the last one to get a taste of their salad. Mrs. Berns looked up just as he brought a spoonful to his mouth.

"Lucille, I believe you've created s-h on a shingle," he said, loud enough to draw the attention of everyone in the room.

Lucille, clearly agitated, tried to smile up at the small gathering while she took the bowl from her husband. Her hands were shaking so badly that she dropped it. It shattered on the floor. "I'm so sorry," she said quietly, her chin quivering.

Hiram glared at her, his eyebrows crossed in annoyance. "Yes you are, Lucille. You're a sorry woman."

Mrs. Berns made her way over to help, shooting eye knives at Hiram as she passed. He made a deliberate show of ignoring the glare.

Mrs. Zindahl clucked and clapped her hands, breaking the uncomfortable mood Hiram's behavior had set. "We've finished early, so we've just enough time for an introduction to my 'Creative Cool Whip' seminar."

Hiram made a noise like a bull. Mrs. Berns glanced up from her position on the floor, where she was kneeling next to Lucille, both of them tossing the glass shards into a nearby garbage can. Mrs. Berns assumed Hiram was making a commentary about the Cool Whip class, something she regrettably had to agree with. Then she saw his face. It was purpling, his eyes bulging. He made the bull noise again, only it wasn't as loud as the first time. His hands clutched his stomach, he doubled over, vomited powerfully, and dropped dead to the floor.

Mrs. Berns had a slight twinkle in her eye as she kneeled next to the corpse in the bright light of the kitchen. "Clearly, it's murder."

"What?" Tabby had run over and was staring into Hiram's dead, open eyes. Her voice was shrill. "Murder?"

Mrs. Berns stood, grabbed a tablecloth from a stack near the door, and covered Hiram and his upchuck. "Yup," she said knowingly, pleased beyond words that this retreat had finally gotten interesting. "I was there for The Great Salmonella Outbreak of 1997. I know food poisoning."

A hush passed through the room. A bad batch of hot dogs had made their way through a certain nursing home system some years before. It was the stuff of legend, and people bragged about surviving it much as they did a tornado or a hurricane.

"I was a volunteer nursing assistant at the time. I was on the front lines."

William, the director, opened his mouth and then closed it, his brilliant smile dimmed. Mrs. Berns read that as permission to take charge. "Given the weapon, we know one of you in this room is responsible, and I have some ideas who. I suggest we finger the culprit before the police arrive and mess everything up. First things first." She placed her hands on her hips. "I want all the Catholics and Presbyterians out of this room. It takes a full-blood Lutheran to turn mayonnaise into a precision killing tool."

The people in the kitchen classroom glanced uncertainly from one to the other, and then began streaming out, careful to avoid the perimeter of the corpse. When those who were going to leave had left, only William, Tabby, Lucille, and the couple who had been standing near the industrial refrigerator remained.

"So," Mrs. Berns said, addressing William. "Wanna tell me what that look you gave Hiram when you first walked in here was all about?"

William couldn't rip his eyes away from the man-shaped tablecloth on the floor. "It's no secret. Hiram and his wife attended last year's retreat. I walked in on him stealing money from the orphan fund jar. I told him to leave the retreat, but instead, he told everyone he'd caught me stealing the money. In the end, it was my word against his, and we had to let the matter drop."

Mrs. Berns nodded. "Revenge. It's a good motive. Do you want to hear an even better one?" She pointed a finger at Tabby, enjoying every minute of this. "Love."

"Me? I didn't love him." Tabby acted surprised, but when Mrs. Berns wouldn't drop her gaze, the woman folded into a puddle of tears. "At least...I didn't want to."

"For shame, woman," Mrs. Berns said. "You don't sleep with another woman's husband, especially when he's such a turd. This affair happened last year?"

Tabby nodded, a fat tear rolling down her cheek.

Mrs. Berns turned her attention to the couple by the fridge. "The two of you didn't look at Hiram even once during this whole class, even though he's been an obnoxious donkey since we started. What's your story?"

The husband ran his hands through his thick silver hair and clenched his fists. "I caught him harassing my wife right before this class. She was leaving the bathroom, he was trying to push her back in. He said it was a misunderstanding. I said I'd kill him if he touched her again."

His wife curled her arm through his and smiled up at him. "He didn't mean it of course. He wouldn't hurt a spider."

That left only Lucille, who'd kept her eyes pinned to the ground since her husband had dropped.

"Lucille?" Mrs. Berns said.

Lucille's eyes flashed up, and Mrs. Berns recognized immediately why the woman had been avoiding contact. Her eyes were currently those of a wild cat, though the fierce emotion drained away as soon as she met Mrs. Berns' glance. Without the momentary fire, Lucille appeared small and gray, a soul-tired woman in her late 70s wearing second-hand clothes and sporting an out-of-date haircut, standing next to the warm corpse of her abusive husband.

"I'm so sorry for the mess," Lucille said, beginning to cry. Mrs. Berns thought the woman was referring to the broken bowl, but then Lucille reached into the cuff of her sleeve and pulled out a Kleenex. A small glass vial immediately dropped out of the cuff and fell to the floor. Amazingly, it didn't break, rather hitting the ground with a soft "tink" and then rolling to the edge of the tablecloth near Mrs. Berns' feet. The insides of the glass vial were smeared with a white cream: the poisoned mayonnaise.

The room gasped. Lucille shrugged, resigned. "He kicked the cat," she said, by way of explanation. "She was the only thing he'd ever treated well, and then last week, he kicked her."

Mrs. Berns studied the five living people in the bright kitchen. Tabby, who'd apparently had her heart broken by Hiram. The married couple, deeply in love and whose sense of security had been ruined by Hiram's assault. The director, who'd had his reputation sullied by the man under the tablecloth. Finally, Lucille, who looked like a dog that had been kicked so many times, she almost forgot how to get up.

Almost.

Outside, the wail of a siren pierced the cool spring air.

"As I was saying earlier, it's clearly murder..." Mrs. Berns cleared her throat. "...for an old lady to lose her husband so late in life, and to something as random as food poisoning." She forced eye contact with each person the room. Every one of them met her stare with a nod, a tiny smile on more than one face. Lucille's expression was one of grateful shock. The corpse and the glass vial lay on the floor between her and Mrs. Berns.

"Let's leave the trash here," Mrs. Berns said, "and go into the non-denominational chapel so that we can all better comfort the new widow."

Mrs. Berns reached down to grab the glass vial. She handed it to Lucille. Then, all five of them stepped around the body and left the Miracles with Mayonnaise classroom.

Mary Logue was born and raised in Minnesota. While she has lived in many other parts of the world—Belgium, France, New York City, and Tucson—she always returns home. She has worked as an editor at numerous presses, including Graywolf Press and The Creative Company, and has taught in MFA programs at the University of Minnesota and Hamline University. She has published ten adult mystery novels (including the Claire Watkins mystery series), four books of poetry, several non-fiction books, and many children's books. *Sleep Like a Tiger*, a picture book, is scheduled for release in the fall, 2012. She lives with writer Pete Hautman in Golden Valley, Minnesota, and Stockholm, Wisconsin.

Murder

Mary Logue

When my sister died
I lost something I've never
found again. Don't even know
what it was.

She was murdered and that's
a terrible thing. What worse
can we do to one another?
Take away the light.

I helped the police
find the man who was
with her when it happened.
He didn't mean to do it.

I don't blame him.
His life had led him to this,
as had hers: tragedy,
great sadness.

I write about murders
and they're never exactly
what anyone wanted.
They happen in the blink

of an eye. No going back.
The losses reverberate
for whole lifetimes.
I miss my sister, always.

CROSSING

There's no murder in this poem.
Only darkness laced with early light,
only working at an old desk, writing lines
that someone might have said in a life

I imagine. And so I live two or
three lives, stories if you will.
They burst on me in the middle of a walk,
they swarm the floor of the office.

The characters, like most of my friends,
do things I would expect
and then not and I'm forced
to enter the story ever deeper.

Often living so many lives is exhausting.
I eat dinner in one and fight in another.
I cry in one and shout in a third.
My me gets eaten up by what might be.

As a tree grows, it branches.
There is a pattern but obscure.
I know the land on the other side of the river.
It is the crossing that worries me.

Lori L. Lake is the author of two short story collections and ten novels, including four books in The Gun Series and two in The Public Eye Mystery Series. Her crime fiction stories have been featured in *The Silence of the Loons*, *Once Upon A Crime*, and *Women of the Mean Streets*. Lori lived in Minnesota for 26 years, but re-located to Portland, Oregon, in 2009. She is currently at work on the third book in The Public Eye Mystery Series. When she's not writing, she's at the gym, the local movie house, or curled up in a chair reading. For more information, see her website at *www.LoriLLake.com*.

An Age-Old Solution

Lori L. Lake

Margo Flynn exited her car and waited. Around the corner, she saw movement and clumped along that direction in oversize tennis shoes. When she reached Jan, her friend and reluctant co-conspirator, she said, "Your car is set for a fast getaway?"

Jan looked stricken. "Yeah, but I don't know if I can do this."

"You can. Don't worry. Just hold my arm—and act old."

"You act old!" Jan whispered.

"We both have to act old, you idiot." Margo hooked her arm with Jan's and concentrated on taking slow steps. She hoped nobody noticed the dowager's hump of a backpack she wore under the enormous scarf she had wrapped around her ancient cardigan. She broke out into a sweat, whether from the layers of clothes or the ridiculous silver wig or nerves, she didn't know.

Jan waved a hand. "Nobody's out tonight. Why don't we make a break for the house?"

Margo said, "We can't. Just walk slow. People don't pay attention to old women. If they do remember later, they'll dismiss us. Hunch over and act like every step's painful."

"Every step is painful with you hanging on me."

Margo loosened her hold and gazed about the neighborhood. She knew her nervous energy was off the chart, but she couldn't help herself.

"I need a cigarette," Jan said.

"Yeah, me too."

"You don't even smoke."

"I might need to after this." Tonight was do or die—or, more accurately, do or pay. And then suffer.

She'd scoped out the neighborhood extensively during the last week, which wasn't as easy as she'd thought it would be because this upscale and trendy Kenwood area in Minneapolis was a busy place by day, but slow in the evening. Few people were out and about after dark, when she most needed to check it out. She hoped she and Jan wouldn't be noticed. Every step Margo took increased her panic level.

A car passed and Margo turned away, toward Jan, as though they were chatting. A dog barked in the distance.

Jan asked, "This asshole doesn't have a dog, does he?"

"No, that'd require him to care about something other than himself. Or at least remembering to feed the pup and take him to the vet. Taddy Detwiler doesn't 'do' love and care. Okay, this is the house—the tan and brown one."

"Holy crap, you weren't kidding. The place is a mansion."

"Uh huh. Complete with a mini-movie theater and an actor's sound stage. Or should I call it a bed stage?"

Jan gave her a quick searching glance, then looked away. Margo knew Jan wasn't happy about this plan, but Margo couldn't think of another way. "We'll pass by and go two doors down. The walkway along the side of that house is covered over with an arbor. No one will see us circle around to the back, and we can cut through to get to Taddy's house."

The backyards were dim and shadowy with only a little ambient light from nearby houses.

Jan whispered, "Nobody's home here?"

"No. Must be on vacation." Or perhaps living in their other homes in the Cayman Islands or Bermuda. The whole neighborhood screamed filthy rich.

Jan let out a muffled grunt as she stumbled. She clutched at Margo to right herself. "I hate these freaky cobblestones."

"Calm down. Take your time." Margo paused, listening. The night noises of cicadas hadn't stopped. She didn't hear an outcry. No lights went on. She had brought along a penlight, but she didn't want to use it unless they really had to. Taking Jan's hand, she steered her onto the lawn.

"I better not walk through dog crap, Margo."

Laughing nervously, Margo led her to the big tan monstrosity where their quarry lived. The house was three-stories high with a foundation at least forty feet wide and fifty feet long. And it had a full basement. Eight thousand square feet for one selfish, mean-spirited creep.

The casement windows along the side were all open as they'd been every night when Margo surveilled the place. Taddy probably thought he was safe because the windowsills were above eye level, perhaps six feet up. Margo unwrapped her scarf and removed the backpack. First she put on latex gloves, then took out a metal contraption and unfolded it. *Snap-snap-snap-snap*...a ladder, hardly a foot wide at the bottom and six inches at the top, clicked into its six-foot height.

"Ready to be my lookout?" Margo asked.

"What if someone comes?"

Margo moved closer and gazed into Jan's worried eyes. "Holler to let me know, then take off over the back fence."

"I won't leave you."

"We don't both need to be caught. Don't risk anything—just run away."

"You sure you want to do this?"

"I have to."

"What if this is the wrong room?"

"It's not. I cased the place way back when. The layout's got to be the same." She put a hand on Jan's shoulder and squeezed. "Get yourself ready now. This'll all be over soon."

As Jan adjusted her old lady slacks and sweater for better mobility, Margo stepped into the flower bed and leaned the ladder against the wall, delighted to see that the legs wedged nicely against the edge of the sidewalk. Jan held the ladder still, and Margo navigated the rungs, careful of her cloddy shoes. She slid the half-open window up as far as it would go and peered into the darkened room. No one in sight, so she inched her way over the sill. It wouldn't do to make a lot of noise, so she took her time.

Once inside, she gave a thumbs-up to Jan, who squatted next to the ladder looking miserable.

While she searched the gigantic wood desk, Margo did a slow burn about its owner. She'd met Theodore Augustus Detwiler—TAD or Taddy for short—her second term in college. He'd acted like a student, but she didn't find out until later that he'd dropped out years before and now spent his time trolling the U of M campus hunting for theater majors to suck into his whirling vortex of shame. She'd been eighteen and naïve, only recently off the bus from Rosholt, South Dakota. A farm girl with the lead roles for *Oklahoma!* and *Grease* on her résumé, she was a sucker for his slick act. He'd wined and dined her, filled her head with stories of fame and grandeur, and made assurances that she was one step away from flying to Hollywood for a screen test.

Thinking back at how stupid she'd been made her shudder.

The nude photos he'd taken early on had been one thing, but the aborted "movie" was something else. He'd worked her like a pimp slowly wears down any good girl, but when the day came to film in the soundproof movie set in his basement, she'd managed to gather enough of her wits to protest. Of course by then she'd disrobed, and some sweaty naked guy had her in a clinch on the "bed stage." She had the sense to refuse to take it any farther. Taddy started out pleading and sweet, graduated to threats, and eventually did everything but hit her. Shaking and unclothed, she made it out of the room with bruises up and down her arms from where he'd manhandled her. Behind her she heard the crew hooting and calling her name.

Fifteen years had passed, and in all that time, she'd never known that the cameras had been rolling. Not until she received a letter at work marked "personal" containing still photos from the "show." She recognized herself immediately—her red hair, pale skin, the birthmark on her right breast. She looked pretty much the same today, just not quite so innocent. On the back was written: "Five grand or this goes to your principal. You have ten days to get the cash together. 50s or smaller. Instructions to come."

No signature, but she knew Taddy Detwiler's writing, even after all these years. She'd wanted to take him out but didn't want to go to jail. Besides, she wasn't the killing kind. She also couldn't see how she could report the blackmail to the police without her employer finding out. It was bad enough that the pictures came to the private school where she worked with third and fourth graders. Thank God no one in the office had opened it! How quickly would they bounce her out of the job using the morals clause if someone saw these photos?

Her only choice was to steal the original photos, movie footage, and any copies—farfetched, she knew, but all she could think to do. Before she received her "instructions," she decided to find out more about Taddy.

So here she was, going through drawers that contained very little: some office supplies, a couple folders of household utility bills, a dictionary. The huge desk was just for show. Taddy didn't even have a computer on it. Giving up on the near-empty drawers, she slithered past the desk, around the expensive leather chairs that smelled like cigars, and paused in front of the wet bar. She wished she could take a moment to slug down a few ounces of liquor from one of the dozens of bottles under the counter. Sober and focused, she told herself.

The room was big enough to serve as both a den and a meeting place for Taddy and his sleazy porn pals. Other than some spendy-looking paintings on the wall and a newer and bigger desk, the room hadn't changed since she'd last been in it.

She wondered if Taddy could still con young girls like he used to. She'd gotten one glimpse of him getting out of his Mercedes the night before last, and all she could think was that Mr. Detwiler should change his name to Mr. Fatwiler. A decade and a half had not been good to him. Besides, everybody and their sick bastard brother could film pornos these days. All you needed was a steady camera hand and a decent video camera, not like in Taddy's heyday when he had an actual mini-movie studio and camera operators who knew how to do all the techie things he was so bad at. Margo imagined that Taddy's income was no longer anything like it'd been in the past, so now he'd turned to blackmail to support his extravagant tastes.

The door to the office was open. She passed through it and crept down the hall. From the other end of the house she heard a laugh track. Taddy had always been a sucker for sitcoms. He was probably hunkered down in the TV room, a giant carbuncle on the butt of humanity, drinking rum and coke. She hoped he'd fallen asleep, but she couldn't be sure, so she retraced her steps and closed the door nearly all the way, not letting it click shut. She hoped what she sought was in the office, not downstairs where the filming used to be done.

She opened the sliding doors to the closet to find a surprisingly large alcove containing a row of six 4-drawer file cabinets and some beautifully crafted built-in shelves overhead and on either side. She clicked on the penlight and scanned the shelves. A couple hundred video cassettes labeled with dates gave way to considerably fewer DVD cases which were not labeled.

"Pssst…"

Startled, Margo spun toward the window.

Jan's chin rested on the sill. "You find it?"

Margo charged over to the window. "Shh. I'm still looking. There's a lot to sift through."

"Well, crap," Jan said. "Want me to come in and help?"

"No, I don't think so. Give me a minute to figure out the system." She went back to the alcove and one by one examined the tapes labeled 1996. Annabel, Alison Q. Alison R. Brianna. Cate. Catherine L. Catherine P. Catherine S. Cathy…and on and on all the way to Willa and Yasmine and Zoe. Where was her name? She skimmed through the 1995 and 1997 tapes just in case something was misfiled. No luck.

Opening a file cabinet drawer, she found that instead of files, it was filled with envelopes crammed with photos. Same with the next cabinet. The third cabinet contained more VHS cassettes, papers, various sized photos—everything stacked in a haphazard manner. She dropped to her knees and dug in the bottom drawer. Some tapes were labeled with numbers, some with dates, and a few with names: Stonehenge. Gooseberry Falls. Leaning Tower of Pisa. Cabot Cove. What? Did he have dirt on Jessica Fletcher? The thought almost made her smile. Were these TV and movie titles? Places they were filmed? She had no clue. The next drawers she opened were in the same shape. How the hell was she going to find her photos and the movie?

Margo sat back on her heels, feeling deflated. This wasn't going to work. She wanted to cry out, to scream bloody murder—or bloody blackmail.

She froze at a noise down the hall. Was that someone humming?

She crawled forward into the alcove and slid one door shut. Before she could reach for the other, she heard noise at the door.

He was going to find her. He would savage her as he had that last time she'd seen him, and he'd add to her torment by calling the police. What about her job, her life? What about Jan? Would Jan be able to get away? Hunched down, Margo waited, hardly breathing.

The door to the office opened. A flash of light from overhead. She pinched her eyes shut. He hummed something tuneless as he walked heavily across the carpet. She heard rustling, a drawer opened and closed. Glass tinkled. He lumbered toward her hiding place. She held her breath and squeezed into the smallest ball she could make. Thud. Something bumped against the wall, and he shuffled off, his humming gradually fading away.

Margo opened her eyes, gasping for air. He'd shut the closet slider. Never looked inside! She slid open the alcove door, drenched in sweat, and panting. The cool breeze coming in through the window gave her a chill. The faint outline of Jan's head popped up in the window frame. Marge staggered across the room.

"I saw him," Jan whispered. "He took two bottles of booze with him."

"Oh, my God. You were supposed to run!"

"And leave you here with that despicable ass? Forget it." She held up her phone. "I put 9-1-1 on speed-dial."

"I can't do this." Margo shook, and her stomach hurt so bad she bent forward a little. Too much adrenalin, too many bad memories, too much fear.

"I'm coming in."

"No, you shouldn't." But she didn't make a move to prevent it. She stood trying to catch her breath. She felt sweaty everywhere and worried she may have peed her pants.

Jan, not quite as lithe as Margo, managed to navigate the window without too much noise and strode over to the alcove.

Margo mumbled, "Now we're both sitting ducks."

"Shut up and give me the light." Jan shone the penlight around the closet. "Holy hell."

"The shit on the shelves has some semblance of order, but the file cabinets don't."

Jan opened a drawer, pulled out a pack of photos, and tucked the penlight under her chin. She fanned the pictures out for Margo to see. "Good God, these are disgusting."

Margo had to agree. The photos she'd posed for fifteen years ago had been rather chaste compared to the spread-eagle pose of the frightened young woman in the shots Jan held.

Jan tossed them back in the drawer, not even bothering to replace them in the envelope.

"Whoa." Margo grabbed Jan's arm. "You don't have gloves on."

She reached for the photos, but Jan held up a hand. "Forget it. I've got a better idea." She pulled out the bottom drawers of all the cabinets and rose. From the bar she grabbed two bottles of booze, opened the liquor, and dumped the contents into the bottom drawers.

"What are you *doing*?" Margo rasped out.

Jan opened the next drawer, allowing the cabinet to tip forward and rest precariously on the bottom drawer.

Margo gripped Jan's shoulder. "We can't do this!"

"Yeah, we can."

Jan got two more bottles of booze and poured them into the drawers and repeated the process twice more. She poured a couple more bottles on the carpet inside the alcove and splashed some against the shelves and wall.

Margo stood frozen, not quite able to take in what she was seeing. Her heart beat so fast that her chest hurt. She thought she might have a heart attack.

Jan held up one last bottle, a specially aged El Dorado Rum. "Go, Margo. Time to get out."

Still rattled and shaking, Margo slipped over the sill. She stood halfway up the ladder, peering in. Jan faced away from her. She bent and Margo heard a sound: *glug-glug-glug.* It echoed in her mind. *Glug...glug...*

Jan backed up to the sill, and Margo slipped down from the ladder. Jan came through the window and paused, her feet on the ladder rungs and upper body still leaning inside the office.

*Snick-snick...*Margo heard a quiet whooshing sound. Fire bloomed inside making the dark wooden walls reflect orange.

Jan closed the window, hopped down, and put her lighter in her pocket. Margo stood staring. What had they done?

"Get the backpack," Jan said. She was already disassembling the ladder. Margo picked up the pack and held it so Jan could stuff the ladder in it. She waited, still in shock, as Jan slipped her arms through the straps and wrapped the scarf around herself.

Jan said, "Come on—let's go!" She dragged Margo through the neighboring yards and around to the sidewalk two doors down.

They paused in the deep shadows next to the house and peeked out toward the empty street.

Margo thought she might throw up. "What if Taddy doesn't get out?"

"Piss on him. Serves him right if you ask me. How many women like you was he blackmailing? How many lives has he ruined?"

"But he could die—"

"Nah, he'll manage to haul his fat ass out somehow. Slugs like him always do."

Whoop-whoop-whoop...

"See," Jan said. "His fire alarm will wake up the dead."

A door opened across the street from Taddy's house. A woman came out on the porch and pointed. She was dressed to the nines in business attire and somehow managed to tiptoe down her front stairs in the highest pair of stilettos Margo had ever seen. Two men came bursting out of the house next door. One held a phone to his ear. The neighborhood came to life before them, little ants emerging from their various anthills.

Margo smelled the aroma of something rotten burning. "How the hell do we get out of here?" she asked.

Jan straightened her tan cardigan and wrapped the scarf tighter. "We're going to wait a few minutes, 'til the fire truck arrives, and then we'll join the horde. After a little while, we'll hobble off."

"Somebody will see."

"Who cares." Jan snickered. "Keep your head down and make sure you act old."

That sounded right to Margo. Jan would go to her car, and Margo would walk stiffly toward hers, and soon this would all be over. She tugged her wig down, smoothing a lock of silver over her forehead, suddenly able to breathe.

A fire truck rounded one corner as an ambulance and police car came from the other direction.

Margo said, "I hope they don't put it out too quickly. That whole alcove needs to be destroyed."

Jan said, "As far as I'm concerned, the entire house better be rubble by morning."

Margo stepped out into the moonlight and said, "Works for me. It couldn't happen to a nicer guy."

William Kent Krueger writes the *New York Times* bestselling Cork O'Connor mystery series. After studying briefly at Stanford University, Kent set out to experience the real world. Over the next twenty years, he logged timber, worked construction, tried his hand at free-lance journalism, and eventually ended up researching child development at the University of Minnesota. He currently makes his living as a full-time author. He lives in St. Paul, a city he dearly loves, and does all his creative writing in a lovely little coffee shop near his home.

Woman in Ice

William Kent Krueger

They watched storm clouds mount the horizon, and under the charcoal threat of that early spring sky, watched Krakauer enter town dragging the woman behind his mule. He said nothing to any of them who stood on the street, their eyes frozen on what the bachelor farmer had hauled to Harrow. He plodded through the village and didn't stop until his mule was abreast of the church, where he finally spoke, calling out, "Whoa there, Abraham." He laid the reins across the mule's neck and took the muddy path through the melting snow to the tiny cottage set back of the church, knocked on the door, removed his flapped cap, and waited respectfully.

The priest, when he appeared, was dressed in jeans and a flannel shirt, dressed in the way of the other folk of Harrow. He seldom wore his collar or cassock unless it was Sunday or he was hearing confessions. He needed nothing to indicate his religious position. He'd been the village priest for twenty years, and those who didn't know him were those who had not yet been born.

"Otto," the priest greeted Krakauer pleasantly and without surprise. He was used to visitors, day or night. He'd kept long vigils at bedsides while his parishioners suffered sickness or the pains of a difficult childbirth or were in need of last rites.

"Come, Father," Krakauer said. "There's something you should see."

The priest grabbed his wool coat from the peg beside the door and followed to where the mule stood before the church. Harrow had gathered there, most of the town, standing in a semi-circle behind Krakauer's beast, eyeing with wonder what the farmer had dragged into their midst. They cleared a little avenue for the priest, and he walked to the great block of ice, which Krakauer had roped to the mule.

The block was roughly three feet thick, three feet wide, and six feet long. The edges were jagged and irregular. The ice itself was as clear as glass. In the center, posed as if in sleep, lay a woman. She wore a white dressing gown, opened at her neck. Her hands and feet were small and bare. Her hair was black and long, tied on one side with a blue satin ribbon, while the other side hung loose upon her breast as if neatly combed. Her eyes were closed, her face pallid but peaceful. She was a woman only barely, not long out of her girlhood. The effect was like the sleeping beauty of that fairy tale, which all people, even those in isolated little Harrow, knew well.

"Where did you find her?" asked the priest.

"With the rest of the ice that's broke up and piled against the lake shore along my property."

Harrow lay at the southern end of a lake so large that, even from the rooftops, the northern shoreline could not be seen.

The priest queried Krakauer again. "Do you know her?"

"Never set eyes on her before, Father."

The priest turned to the half circle of curious faces, all as familiar to him as his own, and asked, "Does anyone know her?"

Given permission, they came closer and looked long at the pale, lovely visage, and although there was sadness in their eyes, there was no look of recognition.

A wind had risen out of the west, rushing at Harrow from the wide emptiness of the Dakotas. With it came the first cold drops of the storm promised by the mounting clouds. The raindrops were mixed with flakes of white.

"Bring her into the church," the priest said.

Krakauer untethered the rope from his mule. The priest opened the door, and several of the men lent a hand hauling the block and the body encased within it into the church. Those who'd been on the street followed as if in a funeral procession, their faces full of both sorrow and wonder. The sound of the ice scraping over the floorboards seemed like a violation of the quiet inside the simple sanctuary, but the priest showed no sign of concern.

"Here," he said, indicating the spot in front of the altar rail where coffins were laid in advance of a funeral service.

The church was cold. The heat stove in the corner was lit only on Sunday mornings before Mass, and the men, as they labored, huffed visible clouds.

Krakauer said, "Someone should go to Dresden and let the sheriff know."

The priest said, "They wouldn't make it before the storm hit, and I would worry about someone out in the blow that's coming. There'll be time enough later."

He faced his congregation, those gathered at the altar rail or standing in the aisle, with a look of assurance, the kind of look they'd seen when he came to their houses to give them comfort in difficult times, and they were prepared to receive his words.

"When the roads are safe to be traveled again, we'll send word to Dresden. In the meantime, I'll keep vigil here and pray."

"Father, do you need company?" Morgan, the blacksmith, asked.

"Anyone who would like to stay and pray with me is welcome."

No one came forward, but neither did they move to leave.

"Your supper tables are waiting," the priest said. "Otto, it's late, and that storm is already on us. Stay in my cottage tonight. Tomorrow you can return to your farm and your animals. You can sleep on the sofa, and there's soup to heat on the stove."

"Thank you, Father," Krakauer said.

The priest turned to the blacksmith. "Will you do Otto the favor of stabling his mule?"

"Of course, Father," Morgan replied.

Slowly his congregation filed out of the church, into the wind, the coming dark, and the deepening storm. The priest went to a closet and took out two candles and brass holders and set them on the altar rail and lit them. Then he seated himself in the first pew, buttoned his wool coat to his chin, and began to pray.

Morgan was the first to arrive. He knocked at the church door, timidly for a man with fists as hard as anvils, opened it a crack, and said, "Father, may I come in?"

"Come," the priest replied from his pew.

The light of the candles, which flickered in the drafts that ran about the little sanctuary, cast the blacksmith's unsteady shadow on the wall as he came forward. He sat down in the pew across the aisle from the priest and stared at the woman trapped in ice.

"I know her, Father," he finally confessed. "You knew her, too. It's my girl, Eva. She ran away five years ago. I never told anyone this, but she left because of me."

The blacksmith put his face in his huge, callused hands, and wept. The priest waited in patient silence.

"Raising her alone, it wasn't easy. I was so hard on her, Father. She was such a pretty girl but so wild. I would catch her sometimes, sneaking in late at night when I thought she was in bed, and I could smell the stink of alcohol on her, and of men. I wanted her to be good. I tried hard to make her good. Sometimes, Father, I hit her because I didn't know what else to do, she vexed me so. And then she ran away."

The man cried so hard that again, for a while, he was unable to speak.

"I've worried about her all these years," he finally said, wiping his nose with the sleeve of his coat. "Wondered where she was and was she safe and was she good. And now here she is, like this."

The priest, who'd known Morgan's daughter well, knew that she and the young woman in the ice were not the same person. They looked nothing alike. But he let the blacksmith go on, because clearly there was a need to confess

"But, Father, she looks so peaceful there, more peaceful than she ever did when she was with me. Do you think she died happy?"

"I think it doesn't matter how she died. I think that she is with the Father of us all now, and how could she not be happy?"

"Do you think she's forgiven me?"

"All that you and I are blind to, she sees now and understands. Like the Father she is with, she forgives everything."

The blacksmith put his palms to his eyes and rubbed away his tears. He stood and stepped to the ice and said to the woman inside, "I love you, Eva. I always did." He kissed his fingertips and touched the ice above her placid face.

"Go in peace," the priest told him.

The wind blew so hard, and the walls of the little church creaked so loudly that the priest barely heard the knock of the next visitor. The door opened and snow swept in, and with it came the grocer's wife. She was a small woman, given to petty miserliness, which didn't go unremarked upon by those in Harrow who owed money at her husband's store. She came forward, hunched like an old woman, though she was barely forty.

"Father," she said. "I heard about this girl. Could I see her?"

Granting permission, the priest held out his hand toward the block before the altar rail.

The grocer's wife stepped close, peered through the clear ice, and in the next instant, fell to her knees. She bowed her head and rocked back and forth and said, "It's a punishment, Father."

"Punishment?" the priest said.

"It's Irma, my sister. My poor little sister. She came two years ago, you remember? I told everyone she was visiting from Saint Paul, but she came to me because she was pregnant and unmarried and needed money. She told me that if I didn't help her, she'd kill herself. She was always given to theatrics, and I didn't believe her, and I sent her away, and I haven't heard from her since. Oh, Father, it's all my fault. What am I to do?"

The grocer's wife was a homely woman, and her sister, Irma, the priest recalled, had been homely as well. The young woman in ice was remarkably beautiful. The priest said, "From this day forward, you will be generous, not only with your family and your neighbors, but with strangers as well."

"I'll do that, Father." She grabbed his hand and squeezed it between her own with painful gratitude. "I swear I'll be the most generous of people. The poor will never have a better friend. Oh, thank you, Father. Thank you."

She left, hurrying outside as if eager to begin a new life.

The doctor came next. He was the priest's age, nearing fifty. The priest was still vigorous, however, while the doctor walked with the pained gait of an ancient man. He came wearing a raccoon coat and a fur cap and carrying his black bag. Although he professed to have no religion, he greeted the priest cordially, in the way of old and equal friends. He kept his coat on against the cold inside the church but brushed its dusting of snow onto the floor and approached the woman in ice.

"I was out on a call at the Henderson farm. Karl got his ribs stove in by one of his horses. Broke two or three. Bad luck for him, good luck for Ursula. He won't be able to lift his arm to hit her for some time."

The doctor leaned over the clear block and studied the body it held.

"One of her satin hair ribbons is missing," he noted.

"Probably lost in the lake," the priest replied.

"Maybe," the doctor said. "But did you notice her neck?"

"What about her neck?"

"A clear bruise line. Strangled, I'd say. Maybe with the missing blue ribbon."

The priest rose and stood beside the doctor and studied the woman.

"What are you going to do about her?" the doctor asked.

"In the morning, when the storm's stopped, someone will go to Dresden for the sheriff."

"Sheriff Blevins?" The doctor made a harsh sound, part snort, part laugh. "If he even comes, he won't be of any use. Doesn't know his ass from his eyeball." He sat down heavily in the nearest pew. "I know most folks around here, but I don't know her. I understand Krakauer found her in the ice piling up at this end of the lake. Could be she drifted over from the other side, from Potsdam. Currents or the wind or something blew her down here. Do you know her?"

"Why would I know her?"

"You get up to Potsdam once a month. Thought maybe you'd seen her there."

The priest's territory included all of the big lake. At the north end was Potsdam, a wild logging and railroad town, full of a lot of rough men and with a number of the kind of women who saw to their needs. Once a month, the priest made the two-day trip by buggy along bad roads to see to the ministrations that were his duty. During a typical two-day stay, he performed several baptisms, at least one wedding, heard a dozen or more confessions, and offered the Holy Eucharist to a handful of the faithful. He stayed in a rooming house and held his services in the back room of a bar owned by a man who, despite the nature of his business, was a devout observer of his faith.

"Nearly a thousand people crowd Potsdam now," the priest said. "They come and go quickly. I know very few, and none of them well. When I'm there, I feel like I'm a stranger in a strange land."

The doctor reached into the pocket of his raccoon coat and drew out a silver flask. "Join me?"

"A cold night," the priest said.

"Aye to that," said the doctor.

They each took a long swallow, then the doctor replaced the cork, put the flask back inside the coat, and prepared to take his leave. He leaned toward the ice block one last time and peered down through the crystalline separation between him and the woman.

"You know," he said with a note of melancholy, "she reminds me of Mary, the last time I saw her."

The doctor was speaking of his wife, who'd died while her husband was away, serving as a surgeon with a Minnesota infantry regiment in the war with the South. He'd never remarried.

"Cholera is not a pretty death," the doctor said. "And so I will imagine her this way." He turned and gave his friend a brief, parting smile, and nodded toward the ice. "Thank you for this gift."

"Not mine," the priest said.

"No, I suppose you'll give credit to that God of yours. Your prerogative. Well, then, I bid you good night and a peaceful vigil."

He clapped the priest on the shoulder in a gesture of familiar goodwill and left.

The storm built in a howling crescendo, and still others came. The butcher's son, who said the young woman was a girl he'd seen on his one and only trip to a city, Fargo, and he'd thought she was the most beautiful thing he'd ever set eyes on. He confessed to the priest that he didn't want to live his life in Harrow, that he wanted to go out into the world and fall in love again and again and have adventures and perhaps write a novel or become painter. Seeing the woman in ice had made him realize that his own life was frozen in a place he could no longer tolerate. He thanked the priest, asked for his blessing, and departed.

The school teacher came. She'd once loved the woman in ice, not, she confessed, as a sister or friend, but with a love full of lust and longing. She was certain the woman had come back into her life in just this way, untouchable, to remind her of the impossibility of such emotion and to confirm that the life she'd chosen for herself, the edification of the young, was her calling and her fulfillment. It was a miracle, a miracle of redemption.

The barber came and the dentist's wife and the milliner and Granny Havlicek, who braved the storm despite her rheumatism.

And near daybreak, the banker made his pilgrimage. The storm had begun to abate by then, and he entered the church wearing no overcoat but looking disheveled and worn, as if he'd not slept a wink. He stumbled to the altar rail and stood above the ice block, breathing hard as that runner at Marathon, and lowered himself to his knees.

"Father," he said. "I need to confess." He lifted his eyes, and they flicked to the little booth in the corner.

"Go ahead, my son," the priest said without rising from his pew. He used the same voice he'd have used if the screen had separated them, a voice he'd cultivated over the years, a tone both encouraging and soothing and that promised no matter the sin, there was always a way to atone.

"I know this woman," the banker said.

"How do you know her?"

"I've known her in the Biblical sense, Father."

"You have lain with this woman?"

"Yes."

"Tell me."

"It was more than a year ago. I was in Potsdam on a business matter and was there for several days. This woman offered herself to me."

"A harlot?"

"No. At least she didn't seem so at first."

"Go on."

"She approached me, Father, as if she'd chosen me. She was beautiful, the most beautiful woman I'd ever seen. I was...flattered. And I'd had alcohol. When our..." He hesitated, looking for a word. "...business was finished, she took one of the ribbons from her hair and ran it down my bare arm until it touched the wedding ring on my finger. She let it rest there and said that if I didn't give her money, she'd make sure my wife knew what I was up to."

"What did you do?"

"I wanted to kill her, Father. Not just to protect me, but to protect my wife and my family and my neighbors. I'm a man of position here. People trust me in ways that are necessary for them. If you can't trust your banker, who can you trust? And her? Who was she? A beautiful face with the soul of a demon. What she did to me, she's done to others, I'm sure. Chosen them and preyed on them, married men or men of position. So I wanted her dead, but I didn't do it. It probably would have been best for everyone if I had. I gave her the money instead, a lot of it, and I told her if I ever saw her again, or if she somehow got word to my wife, I would find her, and I would kill her."

"Why are you confessing to me now?"

"Because now she's here, Father. Like this. Because it's a sign of my sin and my need for expiation. Oh, Father, bless me for I have sinned." He clasped his hands together until he'd squeezed the blood from his knuckles.

The priest gave him a penance, blessed him, and sent him away, saying, "Go and sin no more."

Krakauer woke immediately at the touch of the priest's hand.

"Get up," the priest said quietly. "We have work to do."

In half an hour, Krakauer led his mule to the church. The clouds were gone, and the morning sky was all black ink and star glitter. Along the eastern horizon lay the faintest white promise of dawn. The priest was waiting at the door, and he said, "Bring Abraham inside."

Krakauer looked surprised, but if there was an authority of any kind it Harrow, it was the priest, and so he obeyed. They tethered the ice block to the mule, and the priest said, "Now to the river."

The outlet of the lake was a broad stream south of Harrow. The season was early spring, and although the storm had brought fresh snow the night before, the frozen land had been thawing for some time. As the two men followed Krakauer's mule out of town, the lake called to them in a voice that was the crack and groan of breaking ice. When they neared the river, the sound was overtaken by the hiss of rushing water, the roil of the spring flooding recently begun.

The priest had been quiet, deep in thought. When they reached the river bank, he looked at the water, which was gray in the early dawn and full of great chunks of lake ice. He said, "Let's untie her, Otto."

When the block was free of the rope, Krakauer said, "What now, Father?"

"We put her fate once again into God's hands. Help me push this ice into the river."

Krakauer was dumbfounded, but he did as the priest instructed. Together, they slid the ice block into the water and stood watching as the current carried it away.

"You and I, we will say not a word about this," the priest instructed. "When people ask, we will say only that she's gone. It was a kind of miracle that she came to us, and in the same way, she has left us. Am I clear?"

"Yes, Father. But why?"

"Do you dream, Otto?"

"Sometimes, I guess, Father."

"What do you think of your dreams?"

"Usually they don't make much sense to me."

"We know God as we know a dream, Otto, a dream that often doesn't make much sense but that we all need to believe in. This woman is like that, in a way. She must be gone before we wake to the reality of who she is and who she is not."

Krakauer looked at the priest as if he were talking about one of the holy mysteries of the Church, which the simple farmer had never really understood but had always accepted.

The day had broken fully, the sun just now topping the eastern horizon. The two men stood in the light of the new dawn as the block of ice joined all the other ragged pieces set free by the thaw. Then Krakauer went his way with Abraham, back to his farm, and the priest returned to the village. The streets were empty, and he entered his little cottage without being seen. He set a pot of coffee on to brew, then went to his bedroom, lifted his Bible from the stand in the corner, and brought it back to the kitchen. While the coffee heated on the stove and sunlight came through the window and stretched a long warm hand across his table as if in benediction, he opened the heavy book to a place marked with a long, blue satin ribbon and began to read.

Born, raised and educated in St. Paul, Minnesota, David House-wright is a reformed newspaper reporter and ad man. His novel *Penance* earned the 1996 Edgar Award for Best First Novel from the Mystery Writers of America as well as a Shamus nomination from the Private Eye Writers of America. *Practice to Deceive* won the 1998 Minnesota Book Award and *Jelly's Gold* won the same prize in 2010 (*Tin City* was nominated in 2006 and *The Taking of Libbie, Sd* in 2011). Other novels include *Dearly Departed, A Hard Ticket Home, Pretty Girl Gone, Dead Boyfriends, Madman on a Drum, Highway 61, The Devil and the Diva* and *Curse of the Jade Lily. The Dark Side of Midnight* (St. Martin's Minotaur) will be released in June 2013.

Housewright's short stories have appeared in publications as diverse as *Ellery Queen's Mystery Magazine* and *True Romance* as well as mystery anthologies including *Silence of the Loons, Twin Cities Noir* and *Once Upon a Crime*. He has taught novel-writing courses at the University of Minnesota and Loft Literary Center in Minneapolis. Website: www.davidhousewright.com. Follow him on Twitter and Facebook.

A Turn of the Card

David Housewright

Probably all of his employees thought he was having an affair, that he had a mistress stashed on the top floor of the apartment complex in downtown Minneapolis overlooking the Mississippi River. Maybe his wife did, too. She had been awfully quarrelsome, lately. He wasn't happy about it. Yet it was better that they believed a lie than knew the truth.

He parked his car at a meter on Washington Avenue and walked to the entrance. The security guards knew him. After all, he had been visiting unit 427 at least once a week for the past two years. Yet they made him sign in, anyway, and called ahead before they granted him access to the elevators. He didn't mind. There were cameras in the elevators, outside the elevators and overlooking all the corridors that led to the lofts. There were even panic buttons spaced out along the corridors. He didn't mind those, either.

He knocked softly when he reached 427. The door was pulled open and a young man stepped back to let him pass.

"Good morning, Mr. G," he said.

"Morning, Joe." Mr. G waited while Joe closed the door before he said, "How is she today?"

"Just great, Mr. G."

"Don't give me that, Joe. I asked you a question."

The young man took a deep breath and answered with the exhale. "She's unhappy, Mr. G. She wants out of here. She wants—well, you know."

Mr. G patted Joe's shoulder.

"I know," he said.

"Want me to take off for a while as usual?"

"Be back in an hour."

"Yes, sir."

Joe slipped on his sports jacket, making sure it covered the Beretta he had holstered behind his right hip before he left the apartment. Mr. G slapped the extra dead bolts into place as soon as Joe left and moved deeper into the apartment. His hand brushed the top of a stuffed chair as he crossed the living room. It was an expensive chair. Hell, everything in the loft was expensive. It had cost him $67,842 to furnish it.

"Good morning, Jill," he called. When there was no answer as he moved into the dining room. "Jillian?"

She stepped through the doorway leading to the kitchen carrying a silver serving tray loaded with cups, saucers, spoons, cream, sugar and ornate coffee pot; moving cautiously as if she were threatened by life's sharp edges. Jillian was young, no more than twenty-two he knew, with golden hair that bounced against her shoulders, a fetching figure, and smooth, milky-fresh skin colored with the tint of roses, skin he had seen only in northern girls. Yet it was her eyes that he found most remarkable. They were warm and wide open and so honest that meeting them made a man regret his many sins. And something else—she was the kindest person he had ever met, the epitome of Minnesota Nice.

"We have a French vanilla blend today," she said. "Hope you like it."

"You know I always love your coffee."

She set down the tray and immediately prepared a cup for Mr. G, hesitating before she dumped the second spoonful of sugar into the bowl and giving it a stir.

"You should have less sugar in your diet but I'm tired of arguing about it," Jillian said.

Mr. G smiled as he took the cup and saucer from her outstretched hand. Always thinking of someone else, he thought. He waited while Jillian made her own coffee and then they sat together in the living room. There was some small talk. It bothered Jillian that Mr. G looked so tired these days. He waved her concerns away as he always did.

"How is Joe working out?" he asked.

"I hate him."

"Has he been out of line?"

"No, no. He's—I don't hate him. Joe's been great. Better than the last guy for sure. I just—I hate this. Living like this."

"I'm sorry, Jill. It won't be for much longer."

"That's what you said six months ago. And six months before that. Gene, I feel like a prisoner here, I don't care how much money you're paying me. I want to walk down the street without a bodyguard following me. I want to travel without asking your permission. I want to go back to school. I want to meet men and go out on dates."

"I guess I can't blame you for that, but it's for your own safety. If my competitors knew what you do for me…"

"I know, I know."

"Joe's a good-looking boy."

"C'mon Gene. Joe is terrified of even touching me for fear you'd have him rubbed out. Do gangsters still say that—rubbed out?"

No, they didn't, Mr. G explained, although he was pleased to learn that Joe was keeping his hands to himself. Joe was one of his most trusted employees. 'Course, so was Scott and he lasted all of six days before he started hitting on Jill. Now his job was driving Mr. G's wife. Still, Joe was a young man and Jillian was a young woman and they spent a lot of time together in private—maybe, Mr. G decided, he should remind Joe of his responsibilities before he left.

Jillian set her cup and saucer on the coffee table and stood.

"Should we get to it?" she asked.

Mr. G followed her back into the dining room and sat at the head of the table. Jillian swept the serving tray back into the kitchen. She returned with a glass bowl filled with oil with a small candle floating on top that she set on the buffet and lit with a match. Almost immediately the room was filled with the scent of jasmine. She used the dimmer switch to lower the lights to three-quarters power—setting the mood, she called it. Afterward, she opened a drawer in the buffet and pulled out a deck of Tarot cards wrapped carefully in a red silk scarf. She unwrapped the cards and pulled off the top 22, setting the remaining 56 cards near her elbow.

"I think we'll work with the Major Arcana, today," Jillian said as she passed the cards to Mr. G.

The 78 cards in a Tarot deck are divided into two packs—the

Major Arcana and the Minor Arcana, the word "arcana" meaning "secret" in Latin. Major Arcana is the trump cards. Each has a title and is numbered in Roman numerals I to XXI with one unnumbered card, the Fool. The Minor cards consist of four suits of 13 cards each and except for the addition of "knights," most closely resemble everyday playing cards. Mr. G knew this, along with the Egyptian, Greek, Indian and Chinese origins of Tarot cards, because Jillian had carefully explained it all to him—on more than one occasion. Still, he understood none of it, including why she insisted in calling him "the querent," a phrase he disliked immensely. He only knew that it worked.

Jillian had an uncanny ability to predict significant events in his future, often helping him decide between two alternatives. He had not made an important move without secretly consulting her since he found her dressed like a gypsy and working in a tiny booth at the Stone Arch Bridge Art Festival—emphasis on secretly. Mr. G had become the most influential organized crime figure between Chicago and the West Coast and he was within an eyelash of restoring the criminal underworld that had flourished in Minneapolis until Isadore "Kid Cann" Blumenfeld was finally convicted of a felony—after 25 tries—in 1961. All he needed was a little more time to solidify his alliance with the Outfit. Yet he knew if his competitors and other business associates discovered how thoroughly dependent he was on this young Tarot card reader, he wouldn't last a week.

Mr. G shuffled the cards—the only time anyone but Jillian was allowed to touch them.

"Start with a general question," Jillian advised.

"Will my present business endeavors continue to be successful?"

Mr. G passed the cards back to Jillian. She dealt the top three cards face down in a row in front of her. He understood after so many readings that they represented his past, present and future. Jillian turned over the first card. It was labeled The World and it was reversed. Upside down cards were usually not desirable, Mr. G knew.

"At its very best, the appearance of the World card signals the arrival of your heart's desire," Jillian said. "So even when it's upside down like this, its reversed interpretation cannot be too negative. It usually means that you have chosen wisely in the past, but you still have a way to go before the promised rewards will be delivered."

She turned over the second card to reveal the Chariot.

"Ahh," Jillian said. "The Chariot signals that there are battles to be fought and considerable odds to overcome and that resilience of character will be needed if you are to achieve a victorious conclusion. But, when preceded by the World, the Chariot indicates that the rewards you'll receive will be considerable, although you will take on some very taxing duties in the near future."

The third card—indicating the future—caused Jillian to frown. It was the Wheel of Fortune and it was upside down.

"The Wheel of Fortune reversed like this means there are unpleasant surprises in store for you," she said. "But Gene, you need to know that it's the nature of the wheel to turn and you will find that eventually things will change for the better. However, when the Wheel of Fortune is paired with the Chariot, urgent decisions will be needed to make your luck certain."

"What urgent decisions?" Mr. G asked.

Jillian grinned at him. He had seen the grin before and knew what it meant—"After all these years you still don't get how this works?"

"All right, all right," Mr. G said. "Deal 'em' again. This time use the Minor cards, too."

Jillian joined the two decks together and passed them to Mr. G. He reshuffled them and passed them back.

"What will cause these unpleasant surprises?" he asked.

Jillian dealt the Temperance and Death cards, both reversed, and the ten of Swords. Mr. G knew that the Death card wasn't necessarily a bad thing, although the first time Jillian had dealt it, it scared the hell out of him

"Temperance indicates that you have a rival who competes with you on an emotional and business level; quarrels and strife are likely," Jillian said. "The Death card reversed tells us that drastic changes must be made and when paired with the ten of Swords— Gene, violence comes."

Mr. G stared at the cards for a long time. He was not concerned that there was a rival—"Like that's new," he muttered—or the violence. What concerned him was that the rival was competing with him on an "emotional level." What the hell did that mean, he wondered.

"Another spread?" he asked.

"Of course."

Mr. G reshuffled the cards and passed them over.

"This time be more precise," Jillian said.

"What will be the outcome of the decisions I make?"

Jillian dealt an Ellipse Spread, designed to answer specific questions. The spread was shaped like an arrowhead, with the first and seventh cards at the apexes and the fourth at the point. It expanded the reading, touching on the past, present, future, steps to take, external influence, hopes and fears, and final outcome of the situation. The Fool, three of Pentacles, the Moon, seven of Pentacles, King of Pentacles, seven of Swords and five of Swords—Jillian took a deep breath at the sight of the cards and let it out slowly.

"When I first started doing this, I promised myself if I didn't have anything nice to say to the querent, I wouldn't say anything at all," she said.

"I'm not paying you to be coy with me, Jill."

Jillian dealt three more cards—the Lovers reversed, Ace of Pentacles and five of Pentacles—and took another deep breath.

"Okay," she said. "Now that I have these last three cards, I can tell you I was really concerned, Gene. There is a very strong warning in the original reading that somebody is perpetrating some kind of deceit around you which is potentially quite bad for yourself and your wife. However, the last three cards indicate that you are able to take steps to protect yourself, which is great news."

"Tell me about it."

"In the recent past, you took some calculated risks to improve your position on the material front. On the face, things look very successful. At the moment, you seem to be tying up the last few details connected with it. But it looks to me as though you have not been given all the facts you need to make a good decision. I think you and your wife have been deliberately misled. The man represented as the King of Pentacles appears on the surface to be an honest and helpful associate. However, I am not convinced that he is as straight-forward as he appears. He is definitely a person with his own agenda. These two sevens, they're a little disconcerting, too. The seven of Pentacles tells you that no matter how events may appear, danger lurks and it is important that you be ready to challenge these events through any channel available to you. These last three cards make it clear that as long as you and your wife remain true to each other, you will find the strength to sort things out, although…"

"Although, what?"

"I am concerned by the reversed Lovers. I have no cards here to substantiate what I'm about to say, but the reversed Lovers— Gene, I get the impression that your wife will be more of a hindrance than a help."

Mr. G thought about it for a moment. A hindrance? It was true that they had not been getting along as well lately as they could have, but—he gathered up the cards, reshuffled them, slid the deck in front of Jillian and said, "How will my wife be a hindrance to me?"

Jillian dealt the Moon, Queen of Cups reversed, the Fool, seven of Wands, seven of Cups, nine of Pentacles and the Empress.

"Well?" Mr. G said.

Jillian knew better than to lie to him.

"You have recently discovered some deceit taking place around you," she said. "This appears to be connected to the woman indicated by the Queen of Cups. She's reversed, which indicates— Gene, it indicates a woman who can be immoral and vain, deceitful and perverse, a faithless lover who forces others to indulge her idle whims. However, the Moon can indicate all kinds of deception, including the sort that means things aren't what they seem. Very soon you will be asked to take a risk. This will be quite demanding and you might be tempted to shy away from it. Please don't. Somewhere very close to you is a person who calls himself a friend, but who is running a personal agenda that will do you no good at all. This betrayal will become apparent in the immediate future. And you will be able to pinpoint the individual accurately. Don't be afraid to act. What goes around comes around. Be ready to receive good fortune and happiness. With the Empress in the final position, you'll find love in the air very soon. Just be ready to take the risk when it comes your way."

Mr. G stared at the young woman. God, she was beautiful, he

thought. Was she the Empress? No, no, stop it. What are you think-ing? This is crazy. These cards are wrong.

"Jill, you're telling me that my wife and one of my people are conspiring against me."

"I'm not telling you anything. The cards…"

"The cards? You're expecting me to believe the cards?"

"You always have."

"I want a second reading. Second reading."

Mr. G gathered the cards, shuffled them, gave the deck to Jil-lian and asked, "How will my wife be a hindrance to me?"

Jillian dealt an Ace of Disks, the Fool, Lust, the Tower, Justice, the Sun and the Lovers.

"Again we see uncertainty about something you have recently discovered, with the Tower indicating shock and sudden violence. There is a mention of great and irreversible change, but the same indications that events will very soon re-shape themselves and al-low you a more happy and positive period."

"I don't believe it," Mr. G said. "I don't believe any of it."

Jillian shrugged as she gathered up her Tarot cards and re-wrapped them in the red silk scarf.

"The cards say that all will be revealed to you in the immediate future," she said.

"What's that supposed to mean?"

There was a soft rapping on the door. Joe had returned as in-structed—he had a key, yet never let himself into the loft while Mr. G was in residence. Mr. G rose from his chair and began his departure. Jillian called to him.

"Gene?"

"What?"

"Please be careful."

He nodded at her and yanked the door open, startling Joe and causing him to take a step backward. Mr. G set a hand on the young man's shoulder. There was nothing affectionate about the gesture.

"Listen to me," he said. "Are you listening?"

"Yes, sir."

"Anything happens to that girl in there better happen to you, first. Understand?"

"Yes, sir."

Mr. G retreated from the building, pausing only to sign himself out at the security desk. All the while he considered what the Tarot cards had told him. His wife cheating on him? Sure, they seemed to be going through a rough patch, but that happens to every marriage from time to time, right? And yeah, lately she had been spending a lot of time with her friends. Still, conspiring to betray him with someone in his organization? The cards had always been true in the past but—no, no, no. Not this time. Jillian had screwed up. Or maybe she was just pissed off because he kept her a virtual prisoner in her ivory tower. She had told him once that a true and accurate reading required a calm system and a clear mind. You need to be relaxed. Did Jillian look relaxed to you? Well, yeah, he decided, she did. Yet the cards were wrong. They had to be. After all, who could his wife be involved with? Her driver Scott? Granted, he was unable keep his hands off Jillian...

Mr. G stopped on the sidewalk several yards short of his car. "I don't believe it," he shouted even as he pointed his remote control at the vehicle and pressed the button that opened his locks.

The car exploded.

The force of the blast threw him up against the building.

This betrayal will become apparent in the immediate future, Jillian had said. It was the only thought he held for several moments.

One security guard had hurried to the site of the explosion. The rest had remained at their posts on high alert. They were good boys, Mr. G decided; the kind of boys he wanted in his organization. He returned to 427 without bothering to wait for the police and pounded on the door. It was cautiously opened by Joe who said "Hey, Mr. G. Did you forget something?" Mr. G ignored him, pushing deep into the loft.

"Jill," he called. "Jill, Jill. When she appeared he said, "I need another reading."

He sat at the dining room table in a way that indicated he expected no argument. Jillian gave him one, anyway.

"It doesn't work that way, Gene. You know that. The rule is to wait until circumstances in your life have made a definite change before consulting the cards on the same issue."

"Someone just tried to assassinate me. They put a bomb in my car. How is that for a definite change?"

Without another word, Jillian produced the Tarot cards, un-wrapped the scarf and set them in front of the querent. She did not lower the lights or burn jasmine. Mr. G shuffled the cards and passed them to her.

"How should I deal with the betrayal of my wife and my em-ployee?" he asked.

"Jeezuz," a voice said behind him. Mr. G turned to look. Joe immediately left the room.

Jillian dealt the cards in the Ellipse Spread—the Magician, Death, five of Wands, three of Wands, the Lovers, eight of Disks and the Star.

"You've recently suffered a shocking blow in both an emotion-al and business relationship," she said. "You seem to be express-ing a deep sense of distrust and disappointment. You also seem shaken and disbelieving. In the imminent future there will be a certain amount of conflict, both inner and from outside. You will sometimes feel overwhelmed by the enormity of the events that have taken place and uncertain of your ability to deal with them. I think you will also feel bitter and angry, but if you accept that you're bound to be feeling hurt and then just engage with your hurt, you'll soon be kinder to yourself as you come to grips with this situation. It is important that you make no compromises dur-ing this time. You must be true to yourself. You must follow your code. You'll feel stronger and more clear if you do. In a short time, decisions will be made that will begin to straighten this situation out. Again, it is important that you take care of yourself and make sure your emotional and business needs are attended to. The final card in your reading, in my opinion, is the very best card in the deck. The Star. It promises that your dreams will be fulfilled, your hopes realized, and your aspirations satisfied. It's a beautiful card."

That was all Mr. G needed to hear. He stood abruptly. Jillian also rose from her chair. He took her face in the palms of his hands. He felt like kissing her. He had never done that before. Hell, he thought, he had never even touched her. But that was going to change. Everything was going to change, and quickly. The future she had promised was so wonderful he couldn't wait for it to begin.

Mr. G released the young woman and stepped back.

"Thank you," he said.

He left the loft.

Three days later, Mr. G's wife and her driver were killed in a traffic accident. Or so it was assumed at the time. Acting on an anonymous tip, the police soon discovered the truth and Mr. G was arrested and charged with two counts of first-degree murder. Bail was refused. Joe was the one who broke the news to Jillian.

"He thought his dreams were about to be fulfilled," he said.

"I can't help it if Gene believed all that crap."

"I don't get it. You told me you weren't psychic, that the only reason you were reading Tarot cards at the art fair in the first place was to make some extra money for college."

"That's right," Jillian said.

"Yet everything you told Mr. G in the past two years came true."

"Nah. He subconsciously manipulated events so it seemed to him that my predictions were always accurate even when they weren't. He talked himself into it. That's what true believers do. My old psychology professor called it confirmation bias."

Joe stepped up to Jillian and wrapped his arms around her waist.

"So, now that you can go anywhere you want, where do you want to go?" he asked.

Jillian draped her arms around Joe's neck.

"I thought we'd stay in," she said. "After all, I never did thank you properly for setting the bomb."

Ellen Hart is the author of twenty-eight crime novels in two different series. She is a five-time winner of the Lambda Literary Award for Best Lesbian Mystery, a three-time winner of the Minnesota Book Award for Best Popular Fiction, a three-time winner of the Golden Crown Literary Award in several categories, a recipient of the Alice B Medal, and was made an official GLBT Literary Saint at the Saints & Sinners Literary Festival in New Orleans in 2005. In 2010, Ellen received the GCLS Trailblazer Award for lifetime achievement in the field of lesbian literature. *Rest for the Wicked*, the twentieth Jane Lawless mystery, will be released by St. Martin's/Minotaur in October 2012. Ellen lives in Minneapolis with her partner of 36 years.

Overstuffed

Ellen Hart

Maren Nielsen trudged through the dispiriting drizzle, hands tucked into the pockets of her best wool coat, eyes cast down. Even though she'd worn extra clothing for the graveside service, the cold November wind chilled her to the bone. Dry leaves blew across hard ground as she moved up to the people gathered to say their final goodbyes. The mourners parted as she approached, allowing her to stand closest to the casket. She was, after all, the dearly-departed's only sister.

Raising her eyes to her sister's ex husband, who stood silently on the other side of the coffin, she read his expression as a mixture of guilt and impatience, as if this were merely something he had to get through so he could move on with the rest of his day. Maren didn't even try to disguise the hate in her eyes. *Look at me*, she cried inside, *you pathetic, useless piece of trash*. But, of course, he wouldn't. Their eyes had met only once during the church service. He'd looked away immediately, grimacing, as if her gaze had the power to burn. *If only*, she thought. For what he'd done, she would gladly burn his miserable carcass to the ground.

Bowing her head as the minister intoned his final prayer for Harper's immortal soul, still doing his best to preach a self-declared pagan into heaven, Maren found herself smiling for the first time in days. According to this guy, who'd never met Harper in life, she was in heaven now, looking down on her loved ones, singing God's praises and worshiping at the throne. Maren thought it was more likely that her sister was searching out the heavenly liquor lounge—and a fresh pack of cigarettes. Then again, did any minister ever preach a non-believer into hell in front of the bereaved family members when the father of said family gave significant gifts to the church each year? Harper had lived fast, loved-hard, and died, as she always said she would, young. The police called it a suicide. Even though she had left no note behind, she had terminal cancer, they pointed out, as if it was all a simple equation. There was no sign of foul play, just a cup of tea with sedatives dissolved in it and a syringe with a clear thumbprint belonging to Harper.

Maren was grateful when the service was finally over. Feeling a hand slip around her arm, she looked up to find her father gazing down at her. "You okay?" he asked.

"Yeah, I guess. How about you?"

"Holding up. Are you coming back to the church for the reception?"

"I don't know, Dad. The idea of standing around talking to a bunch of people I've never met...it just doesn't feel right. All the people I care about were at my house this morning."

"I get it," he said, pulling on his gloves. "You do what you need to do. Me, I've got to keep busy. I knew we didn't have much time left with her, but I didn't think it would end like this." His eyes filled with tears and he looked away. "We'll need to get together soon. Since she was living at your place for the better part of the year, we'll need to look through her papers—unless you've already done it."

"I've gone into her room a few times, but I haven't touched anything."

He drew her protectively into his arms. "We'll get through this."

Maren spent the rest of the afternoon driving around, cruising past the house where she and Harper had grown up, their grade school, middle school, and high school, the bushes where Harper claimed she'd lost her virginity, her favorite watering hole, the mini-mansion where she and Richard had lived before their separation— where Richard still lived with his soon-to-be trophy fiancé. It was hard to keep the bitterness at bay. She'd never liked Richard, never understood what Harper saw in him. Sure, he was a rich doctor, but Harper had never been all that interested in money. He was smart, which probably impressed her. He was certainly good looking enough—blond, Nordic, with an athletic grace that belied the fact that he was fifteen years older. If Harper had a weakness, it was for IQ in a pretty package.

Maren wished now that she'd spent more time with her sister. She'd been hoping that, when Harper moved in, they would become close again, the way they'd been as kids. Sadly, it never happened. Harper was an emergency room nurse. Even after several rounds of chemo, she still worked her regular hours. She said she loved her job because it was difficult and intense—she was always in the middle of some drama. Maren, who worked equally long hours as an exhibit designer at the Minnesota Science Museum, couldn't imagine wanting to spend each work day surrounded by such suffering and misery. Different strokes, she thought, in her more egalitarian moments.

As the afternoon light began to fade over the University of Minnesota—Maren's final destination on her drive down memory lane—she returned to her house, a small bungalow in south Minneapolis. Entering through the back door, she turned on a light over the kitchen sink and took off her coat, dropping it over the back of a chair. Feeling a chill that had nothing to do with the temperature, she flipped on the gas fireplace in the attached family room, warming her hands next to the blower as the blue flames danced behind the glass.

Oil and water, she thought. That's what she and Harper had been. And yet, in one important philosophical way, they had been alike: both believed in *something* after death—that the grave wasn't the end. They'd discussed it late one night a few weeks back, Harper promising that, after she was gone, she'd find a way to tell Maren all about it. Since they were already half in the bag, the comment had caused some snickering, eventually outright laughter. Harper had refilled their martini glasses, then kicked back and continued to talk about the life she would lead on the other side.

All Maren could remember thinking was, how many times had people made that sort of ridiculous promise to each other, and who had ever come back to tell the tale?

Hearing the front bell chime and assuming it was her father, Maren rushed through the house to answer it. Pulling open the front door, she found Richard standing outside.

"Well? Are you going to invite me in?" As always, he used his deeply rational, infuriatingly calm doctor voice.

"I'm not sure."

"Come on. It's starting to sleet."

"Is Pamela with you?"

"She's in the car."

Maren glanced over his shoulder, seeing a shadow inside his Mercedes. She unlocked the screen and stepped back, but only a few feet. There was no way she would let him come all the way in.

He removed his hat, held it in his hands. "I think we need to clear the air. I've heard some scuttlebutt around the hospital—rumors started by you. I'm not happy, Maren. I also saw the way you were looking at me at the funeral and I didn't appreciate it."

"Boo freakin' hoo."

"You and Harper—you both have smart mouths on you. Makes me realize how much I don't miss her."

"Nice, Rich. Always the class act. I mean, how many men are there who would learn about their wife's cancer one week and the next ask her for a divorce?"

"It didn't come out of the blue."

"Right. Tell me exactly when you met the skank you're currently living with?"

He made a fist, shoved it in her face, then thought better of it and pushed his hand into the pocket of his coat. "Okay, so you hate me for leaving her. To quote you—boo hoo."

"I hate you for way more than that." Her emotions had finally come to the boiling point. "I know what you did. The police may think Harper's death was a suicide, but I know better."

"You don't know anything."

"You came to visit her the day she died."

"Who told you that?"

"Are you denying it?"

With a quick, slanting glance, he said, "No. I was here. So what? We had a lot to talk about."

"You mean the divorce settlement. You weren't getting all you deserved, were you? She told me she wanted what she wanted, and refused to negotiate on your terms."

"I was being completely fair."

"Sure you were, Rich. We all know how fair you can be."

Glancing down at his wet boots, he said, "What do you want from me?"

"How about the truth. You were the one who brought the syringe. You dumped sedatives in her tea, then gave her the overdose that killed her."

His head popped up like he'd been slapped. "Why would I commit a murder when all I had to do was wait until the cancer took her? You must think I'm a moron."

"I think you're *absurd*, Richard. A walking, talking cliché. Oh, and you can add arrogant and entitled to the mix, too. You assumed you could get away with it because you're so much smarter than everyone else." Someone needed to point out to him that arrogance, locally known as The Big Head, was frowned upon in Minnesota. "You're also impatient," she continued. "Harper...she might have lived for another year—or even two."

"And made my life miserable every single day."

"You admit it then? You did it?"

"Oh, get real. Of course not. There's no way on earth you could prove an allegation like that."

"So it was the perfect murder?"

"If I *was* going to commit a murder, you can believe I'd be smart enough to pull it off without getting caught. Don't bother looking for clues. There aren't any." He allowed himself a small smile. "Harper was depressed. She told me she was thinking of packing it in."

"That's a lie."

"You're saying she wasn't depressed?"

"I'll tell you what she told me. When death came, she wanted to meet it head on. Awake, if possible, looking it square in the eye. She wasn't afraid. But she also said that, for whatever time she had left, she would live it on her terms."

"None of that negates the possibility of suicide."

"She promised me she would never do that and I believed her."

"You can't put stock in what a terminally ill, depressed woman says."

Maren found her resolve crumbling. "Get out."

"Gladly. But just so that we're clear, if you continue to badmouth me, to say I had anything to do with her death, I'm going to take legal action against you."

"Out," she said. She picked up an umbrella and thrust it at

him, scaring him enough to force him backwards out the door.

Once she was alone, she broke into tears and crumpled onto the couch. The house felt so empty without the promise of her sister coming home. On a night like tonight, they might eat together, watch a show on TV. Most of the time, however, they spent their evenings apart. Maren liked to go out. She had lots of friends and would often make a date to have dinner or take in a movie. On other nights, she would meet a friend for a drink. They'd relax and process the day. At one of the bars in question, she'd become friendly with the owner. She liked him a lot, and kept hoping he'd ask her out.

Harper never left the house at night anymore. She'd begun work on a memoir, which, she pointed out, was for her eyes only. She was writing it to make sense of her life, to put things in perspective, to help her understand, as she faced death, what she'd never been able to understand during the rush of life.

Wiping the tears off her cheeks, Maren sat back, gave a sigh full of regret, then kicked off her shoes. She hadn't eaten much today and figured she should probably fix herself a sandwich, but the heaviness inside her, both body and soul, made it impossible to move. Next to her on the end table was a pack of Harper's Virginia Slims and a Bic lighter. Maren didn't smoke, but on a whim, she lit one and then, in the growing darkness, watched as wisps of smoke curled and shifted, coiled and swirled back on themselves. She was so mesmerized by the sight that she almost missed the insubstantial form that moved out of the kitchen holding a glass of bourbon in one hand and a cigarette in the other. Maren blinked, cleared her throat, and then shook off the vision. It was a ritual she'd seen so often in the last few months that her mind had to be playing tricks on her.

Most evenings, her sister would pour herself that bourbon, light a cigarette, and head up the stairs to tap away on her laptop in the small room she'd made into a study. Those days were over now. No matter how hard she tried to conjure up her sister's image, that's all it was. A phantom. A longing.

Stubbing out the cigarette, Maren rose, feeling exhausted and full of gloom. She hesitated at the bottom of the steps, flipping on the second floor light and listening. She wouldn't admit it out loud, but something about being alone in the house at night, walking up those narrow, badly lit stairs, had always unnerved her.

"Harper?" she called, knowing she was being silly.

She might hope for life after death, but that didn't mean she believed in boogie men. She had good locks on the doors and windows, so there was no reason to be afraid. She reassured herself, feeling like she was five years old, as she trudged up to the second floor bathroom to run herself a bath.

As she walked down the hall, she saw that the door to her sister's study was closed, just as she'd left it. Opening it a crack, she was baffled to find that the little red dot on Harper's laptop was glowing in the dark. She flipped on the overhead light, sure as she could be that she'd turned the computer off days ago. Then again, so many people had been in the house this morning—relatives and friends who might have used it to check their email, kids on the prowl for something to do other than sit in the living room with the grieving adults and try to act sad.

Maren supposed she could take a quick look at what her sister had been writing, though it would likely make her feel too much like a voyeur. With a sudden burst of solidarity, she decided to delete it. Sitting down at the desk, she felt tears burn her eyes as she pressed a key and watched the file vanish.

"If you're here, say something," she cried out.

She glanced around the study, taking in all of Harper's beloved stuffed animals: The series of hand puppets lined up on top of a bookshelf; a stuffed pink and white elephant that rested next to her iPod sound system; a fuzzy stuffed bat that hung from the ceiling; and Harper's most beloved overstuffed teddy bear, Boris, who sat in their grandmother's old rocking chair in the corner.

"Richard was just here," Maren said less loudly. "I accused him of murder. Felt good. He's such a slime. Good thing he left Pamela the skank out in the car." Picking up a pen, she tapped it against the side of the laptop. "I know, I know. Go with the flow. Go where the universe takes you. Quit trying to direct the movie yourself." Disgusted, she pushed out of the chair. "In case you want to talk, I'll be in the bathtub. Hope you're having as much fun as I am." She shut off the laptop, turned off the overhead light and closed the door. "Is this how our communication works now?" she called as she moved on down the hallway. "I talk and you listen? *Not what I expected*," she shouted. "*Major disappointment.*"

After a fitful night's sleep, Maren rose around nine the next morning. On her way down to the kitchen to make herself some toast and coffee, she walked past the door to her sister's study. She looked in and saw that the laptop was on again.

"What the hell?" she whispered, feeling a shiver roll through her.

Moving warily up to the desk, she saw one short sentence blinking at her.

Hug Boris for me.

As if in a trance, Maren lowered herself into the chair. She read the sentence over and over, wondering what the hell was going on. "Harper?" she said, glancing around the room, feeling deeply creeped-out, and at the same time, utterly fascinated. Seeing the oversized stuffed bear smiling at her from the rocking chair, she got up. His plaid sweater had grown scruffy and his fur was threadbare from being hugged so much, loved so hard, for such a long time. As she picked him up, something heavy fell from a slit in his back.

There on the rug at her feet was a small, digital video camera.

Still holding Boris, Maren bent to pick it up. She sat back down, propping Boris up on the edge of the desk. She hit the play button on the camera and a menu appeared on the screen. She started the recording from the beginning. Up on the tiny screen came a picture of Harper and Richard.

Maren drew in a breath. This was the last thing she'd expected...and yet, it made a certain sense. Most likely, Harper had wanted to insure that her lawyer and an eventual judge would get a first-hand look at the sort of bullying tactics Richard used on her in private. Instead, she'd recorded her murder.

In the picture, while Harper's back was momentarily turned to dig a file folder out of the bottom drawer of her desk, Richard had stirred something into her tea. He remained uncharacteristically civil as they discussed one of the biggest issues in the divorce settlement—who would retain ownership of the cabin on Lake Superior. It didn't take long before Harper's words grew garbled. Once she'd slumped in her chair, Richard snapped his fingers in front of her face a couple of times, then injected her with the overdose of morphine. Before pressing her hand around the syringe, he wiped off his fingerprints. He stood for a moment, gazing down at her.

"Look what you made me do," he said, his voice moving from whisper to shout. "I never wanted this. I warned you. I told you if you messed with me you'd regret it." Moving around the room, he snarled, "I don't know how you stand all this toy crap. It's like living in a bad F.A.O. Schwartz commercial." Glaring briefly into the camera in Boris's tummy, he whirled around and shoved a finger at Harper's lifeless chest. "I'm not a monster. If only you hadn't been so pigheaded! This is what it comes down to. You get nothing. And me, I get it all, just like I told you I would."

Maren covered her mouth with her hand. Pulling Boris into her lap, she hugged him tight and whispered, "Not for long, Richard. *Not for long.*"

A one-time innkeeper with a taste for adventure, Elizabeth has been a private pilot, sky diver, scuba diver, and liveaboard sailor. Extensive travel in the US, Canada, Mexico and Europe led to a second career as a free-lance travel writer, during which she began writing a series of police procedural mysteries set in southeast Minnesota, where she grew up. Her books contrast the sometimes gritty routine of police work with the idyllic rural scenes around a mid-size city in the upper midwest. In 2007, she inaugurated the Sarah Burke series with *Cool in Tucson*. Now with Severn House, she alternates between the two. Latest Minnesota title: *The Ten-Mile Trials*. Latest Tucson mystery: *The Magic Line*.

The Butler Didn't

Elizabeth Gunn

"We're in the middle of Act Three," Rosalie said. "All the action for the next couple of pages concerns tea. There has to be tea. So when the butler didn't come in—" The uniformed policeman touched her elbow. She shook him off impatiently, but the detective nodded to him, and the officer took her arm firmly, saying, "*Now*, Miss." She sighed and tossed her lovely head, but nobody came to her rescue, so after a few more dramatic sighs she went with him.

"We improvised," the director said, completing her story. His name was Fred, and every cast member seemed to have a different pet name for him, Freddie or Fritzie, even Fob, which made no sense till the detective noticed his full name on the playbill: Fred O. Berryman. "I dropped some pots backstage." He pursed his lips ironically. "Made a great crash so Rosalie could look puzzled for a moment, and then kind of mug the audience and say, 'Well, *somebody* needs to bring tea.' I staggered on with a tray full of cups, and the audience just *loved* it! We got the biggest hand of the season so far."

"Which isn't saying much." William said. "*Agnes of God* really bombed." William was this summer's Algernon in *The Importance of Being Earnest*, the current production and a staple for one week every year.

"It may be hackneyed but it draws summer people," Fred said. "The wives want to be seen supporting the local arts community, and the husbands say, 'Pick a night when it's not Shakespeare or anything heavy, and I'll go.' So they come for silly old Earnest and, sometimes, even stay awake."

The officer came back and led William to another room. The detective had called them all back to the stage, where the story started, but he wanted to interview them separately. His nametag read: D. Blake, Detective, MPD. D for David, M for Minneapolis. He didn't want civilians calling him anything but Detective; he kept his distance, polite but, he hoped, somewhat intimidating. A black belt but only five feet nine inches tall, he had given some thought to his persona.

"You knew the butler wasn't going to come on?" the detective asked Fred. "You'd had time to plan that?"

"Well, yes, just barely," Fred said. "We kind of punted through the servant part he didn't show for in Act One, and I told everybody at the break, 'Quick, help me figure out how to cover this tea business in case he doesn't make it in at all.'"

"He was unreliable,"—glancing at his notes—"this Jeffrey Thronson?"

Two actors who'd just come in smirked silently.

"Well, late sometimes," Fred said, "but he's never missed a whole performance before." The officer came back and led the newcomers away.

"Of course, I didn't know him very well," Fred added.

"Jeffrey wasn't a local?"

"No, he just, um, graduated from William and Mary. Well, didn't graduate, I guess. Dropped out. Two years ago, actually."

"Two *years*?" The detective made a little sound, like *shee*. "What's he been doing since?"

Fred shrugged. "Drifting, I guess."

"But you took him on for the season anyway?"

Another shrug. "That's what we do. Try people out." Fred's attention seemed to be drifting, too.

"His name is the same as one of the sponsors on the playbill, I notice."

"Not a coincidence. Jeffrey is Elliott Thronson's nephew." Fred's expression remained bland, but his voice cracked on "Thronson." *Director's an actor too*, Blake decided.

"Thronson Auto is a sponsor of the theater?"

"Indeed. The biggest one." A shadow, like a cloud crossing the sun, before the amiable mask slid back in place. "He's been very good to us. And Jeffrey was generous too, always buying drinks and offering rides in the cream-puff car. Michael's happier I notice."

He couldn't resist a malicious wink.

"Who actually reported Thronson missing? You?"

"No. Didn't his uncle call it in?"

"I don't know. That's why I'm asking."

"Anyway his uncle's the responsible party." The detective raised his eyebrows, and Fred amended, "I mean, because of Jeff's legal age. Supposedly Jeff was out here because he couldn't keep his laces tied in New York…"

"What does that mean, 'keep his laces tied?'"

"Well…he'd wandered off a couple of times. His mother said he was losing focus. So she sent him to her brother, to find him something *meaningful to do*."

"And Thronson brought him here so you'd, what, make him an actor?"

Fred was peering into the corner now, as if the corner might hold printed instructions telling him what to say next about Jeffrey Thronson.

"You know," he said finally, as if he'd found the pamphlet, "I really think you ought to talk to Mr. Thronson before you go any farther with this."

"Fine," the detective said, and surprised everybody by walking out the side door of the theater, nodding to his deputies and not even sparing a glance for the actors sitting around waiting for him.

Not used to being ignored, they all began chattering like sparrows, wanting to know where he'd gone and when he'd be back. William said this was ridiculous, he had nothing to say about this bit player he hardly knew, and he had places to go. Haley, the officer escorting the actors, said, "I can't release you until the detective gets back."

William, playing belligerent—he had been doing pilates, beefing up, and felt he had the macho voice nailed—stood up with his biceps at full flex and said, "What's this release bullshit? Am I under arrest?"

"Not yet," Haley said. He didn't have to play it cool because every inch of him, from his cowlick to his bunions, had been icy cold ever since a storefront firefight eight days ago. He was longing to get a little warmth back into his life, but obviously this bugger wasn't going to provide it. His calm hazel eyes regarded the actor the way a biologist looks at a fruit fly. After a good look at Haley's face, William sat down slowly and stayed quiet.

In the backseat of a luxury sedan around the corner, Detective Blake talked to Elliott Thronson.

"Bringing tea isn't the only thing he didn't do," Thronson said. "He didn't attend the remedial reading class I enrolled him in and paid for. He didn't pay his room rent, though the theater was paying him a living wage for doing very little, and I suspect his mother was sending him money, too, after she promised not to." He shrugged, irritably. "I had to write his landlady a check before she'd give me the key. And when I got inside I was sorry I came."

"Big mess, huh?" Blake, who saw a lot of messes, wasn't interested in the details. "Why did you? Go there, I mean."

"Because they told me he was missing."

"Who did?"

"That director. I think. Does it matter? I thought that's who was calling me. He has that kind of a mincy voice. 'This is the theater,' he said." (His imitation wasn't perfect, but effectively suggested Fred O. Berryman) " 'And I wonder if you know where your nephew is.' As if I had nothing better to do than chase around looking for my hapless nephew," he burst out. His hands performed an endless dry wash of frustration.

"So you didn't find him in his messy room, but you eventually did find him."

"Unconscious in his car. After searching for over an hour." Something about that answer gave him a shuddering fit of—what? It looked like guilt, but who could blame him for taking a while to find the pricey car his nephew was trying to keep hidden?

"In an alley downtown. Then you called the police." It was all in the record, but Blake thought if he got the man to say what he did, he might explain why he felt so bad about it. "I'm curious why you did that if you thought he was just passed out."

"Well I—I'd promised his mother we'd handle him, keep everything private, but it looked too complicated for James and me to deal with." He nodded at the neatly uniformed chauffeur standing by his hood ornament. "Blood all over him and the car, and vomit…" He turned his face away. "James is a loyal employee, none better, but you only keep people like him by knowing the limits of what to ask for." He had uttered an axiom, and, for a moment, it almost calmed him down.

"So you figured you'd let the police clean him up." Could Thorson's guilt be as simple as that? Anyway the question might put him on the defensive and maybe that would get him to say what was eating him.

Now Thronson sprang to his own defense. "And figure out what was *wrong* with him, because…I'd seen him just that morning! He seemed fine then, but there he was, sprawled in the backseat, out cold! I didn't know…"

"Was the car unlocked?"

"No, but I had the extra key."

"The extra…"

"It's my car. I let him use it while he was here. I always say, never loan a car; it always leads to hard feelings; and Jeffrey just proved me right again! A mess all over my nice Mercedes, the GPS missing…"

"His wallet's gone, too. Or do you have it?"

"Good Heavens, no, why would I take his wallet? The less I know about what's in there, the better. So he was robbed? Somebody killed him for trinkets?"

"And then locked the car? Unusual." They stared at each other for a moment before Blake said, "Well, so you called the police and said what?"

"Said I've just found my nephew, he's unconscious in my car, can you help me? They asked me, 'Are you sure he's unconscious? Did you try to wake him?' and I said 'Of course I tried. I shook him and he didn't respond.'

"So then they sent an *ambulance.*" Thronson's perfectly groomed face was turning red. "I could hear the sirens coming for miles! This huge truck wheeled up, people in scrubs leaped out with stethoscopes, and"—shaking his head—"in a couple of minutes they told me, 'We can't get a heartbeat so we're going to Emergency,' and that siren screamed again all the way to the hospital. It was intensely embarrassing. People staring…"

"Ah, embarrassing." Briefly pleased, Blake described the many tests still to be done and said he'd be in touch.

Back inside, Blake interviewed the two actors he hadn't spoken to before, a pair of androgynous identical twins in their early twenties, slender and fey. Their value to the troupe, they said and Fred agreed, was that they were extremely adaptable, could play any part in any play, both genders, any accent, and were quick studies. "So we understudy all the parts, including each other's," Barry said.

"We can play Nick and Nora," Harry added, "and switch wigs and play the opposite parts in the second act. No one will even notice."

They had a roaming habit, wandering casually around the room while they answered questions so that Blake was never able to watch both of them at the same time. He thought they had the distraction techniques of pickpockets. He asked them to hold the two ends of a short cord while French, the young detective who was helping him with the case, measured every inch of their bodies. Blake didn't care about the quarter-inch difference in height French reported, but he was able to watch the identical glint of contempt in both handsome faces when he asked them how they got along with Jeffrey Thronson.

"The rich boy didn't bother with us," Harry said.

"Hardly spoke two words to us, actually," Barry said. "And we left him alone, too."

"You didn't party with him, take rides in the Mercedes convertible? Something about him you didn't like?"

Barry shrugged. "He was just...the uncle's baby, you know? Better to give a wide berth."

"Besides we're always so busy when a play's running," Harry said. "Just now in *Earnest* I'm playing the reverend, the gardener, the solicitor, and, now, sometimes the servants."

"Sometimes?"

"Depends how many volunteers show up."

"And I'm playing Lady Bracknell and the governess. Remember the night I mixed up the wigs?" Barry asked his brother, and the two collapsed onto a sofa in a brief fit of hilarity.

Not trying to hide his impatience, the detective called the theater company together and told them, "Well, there's a lot of work to do yet. Autopsy's today, then there are tox screens, DNA tests, fingerprints, all that takes longer. Till I get those results, please," he said gravely, "stay in town and keep yourselves available for further questions." He put as much weight as he could into the request, knowing he didn't have enough evidence to make it a demand.

"Well, I've tested for a couple of movies," Rosalie fretted, pushing her perfect curls around. "What do I do if they call? Surely you don't expect me to blow off a movie offer just to talk about a bit player I hardly knew."

"Call me if you get an offer," Blake said, "and we'll discuss it." He'd lost interest before he finished the answer, distracted by the twins' reaction to Rosalie's last statement. He found them hooting over a game on a Nintendo 3DS, and asked them, "All that surprise at Rosalie's answer and then the smirking, what's that about?"

"Not to tattle," Harry said, quivering with the joy of doing just that, "but Rosalie saying she hardly knew the deceased is so silly. We all knew they were canoodling from Jeffrey's first day here."

Barry nodded. "Rosalie'd fuck a dog if he had a big enough allowance."

"Especially if he kept talking about going to Hollywood and starting his own production company," Harry said, and added good-naturedly, "as who among us would not, if the story seemed at all credible?"

"You didn't think Jeffrey was serious?"

"Serious? We didn't think he was even quite tethered to this planet."

"So you weren't competing with Rosalie for his attention?"

The twins looked at each other and sighed. Barry said, "Again," and Harry nodded. Harry told Blake, "We're slim and neat with nice hair, and we work in theater. But Mother Nature is a tricky old broad, Detective, and it turns out we are immutably heterosexual. Sorry to disappoint you."

"Oh, comes to suspects," said Blake, who disliked being condescended to, "I don't really have a preference one way or the other."

"Ah," Barry said. "Good to know." He met his brother's eyes, and they walked out of the room together, quiet for once and not playing any games.

A twenty-first-century criminologist collects analyses from many scientists, and cobbles them together with the truth-telling and fable-spinning of various witnesses. Finally he makes an informed guess that he can get most of his evidence to support, and gives it to the lawyers to prove—or not—in court.

It's a slow business. Four months later, getting ready to hand over the case to the county attorney, Blake still had questions to clear up. He began calling his witnesses into the station one by one, talking to them in the little interview rooms where the conversations could be videotaped.

He asked Michael, the well-built wannabe hero, "Why did you say you hardly knew him? I have a dozen witnesses who'll swear they saw you together every day."

"I'm not the only one," Michael said, turning whiny. "Rosalie—."

"Never mind her! Just tell me what you were doing for Jeffrey that you don't want me to know about? What was he paying you to do?"

"What makes you think—oh, hell." His broad shoulders shrank a little as his resistance crumbled. "You know, don't you? How do you always know?"

"We get paid to know," said the detective, who didn't, not quite yet—but Michael led him to it. Soon he had the name of the dealer and Michael's pledge to make one more buy. "Then you can forget this whole thing," Blake said kindly. "I'm not a narc. I'm People Crimes."

Rosalie was even easier. Blake told her, "I didn't care that you were sleeping with the new boy, till you made such a point of denying it. Why bother?"

"When I have so many loyal friends here who are eager to snitch, you mean?" She tossed the beautiful curls and flounced.

"Life's a bitch, isn't it? Answer my question."

"Minneapolis isn't L.A. This audience likes us to be, you know, Minnesota nice. And murder...this is going to get ugly."

"Did I say he was murdered? I don't think so."

"Well—"

"Maybe you think that because of the blood we found on the handle of your kitchen knife. The DNA matches both of you, and the blade fits the size of his wounds." Little wimpy cuts that could be made by any paring knife, not fatal but they'd drawn enough blood to make her think so.

"He was hurting me!" She had started to cry. "I thought at first he was my dream guy, handsome and rich and wanted to act. I thought I could help him and we'd...but he turned out to be so sick." Her nose ran; he passed her a box of tissues. "The drugs... when he got all he wanted he got brutal! I didn't mean to kill him, truly!" She grabbed more tissues and buried her face. "I was just defending myself! But he fell on the floor and I couldn't move him. I had to call the twins to help me."

"Lucky they came, huh?" He got up. "You sit here and think if there's anything more you want to tell me, and I'll be back."

He tackled the twins next—almost literally, because they made him angry, wanting him to wait while they finished a game. He put them in separate rooms and had French monitor the interviews. "Thought you were so smart with the gloves and all," he told Barry. "But you sweat plenty getting him into that car, and sweat carries DNA just as well as blood does."

"I don't sweat," Barry said, playing snooty, "I perspire."

Blake cut to the chase. "I know about his GPS on eBay, and his watch at the pawn shop. How much cash did you get?" They were both sure they'd wiggle away from the money, which was, after all, cash. But a snitch had told him Harry's gambling debt was satisfied, and Barry's ex confirmed he was current at last with child support. "Nice haul, and I can prove most of it. Thieves should pay attention to public records."

"He had plenty more where that came from," Harry said. "And he was alive when we left him."

"In a dark alley," Blake said, "and called Thronson, pretending to be Berryman." He left them in the claustrophobic boxes while he interviewed Elliott Thronson, the only one of the group who admitted blame.

"I'm desperately sorry it took me so long to find that car. If I'd been quicker, who knows? Maybe we'd have saved him."

"Yes, tragic," Blake said. Thronson watched in astonishment as the detective got up suddenly, looking angry, crossed the large interview room where they'd been sitting, and told French, "Get all those other people in here."

"If I wasn't so busy I'd arrest every last one of you," he growled at them when the whole company was assembled. "You're all guilty of lying to the police, do you think that's a joke? Wasting my time? Fortunately experience has taught me not to believe half of what I'm told!"

"Really, Detective," Thronson said, "why are you so..."

"You're the worst of all, in a way," Blake said, "all this sensitive bullshit about 'if only I'd been quicker.' You don't think I know you've got a tracker on that car? What were you really doing for that hour and a half before you called 911?"

Elliott Thronson turned away, turned back, and finally said in a small voice, "Fighting with my sister. Shameful! But I lost my temper when I saw what Jeffrey had done to my car. I phoned her up and just ranted. 'How many more times in my life am I going to have to clean up your messes?' She yelled back and then cried. It all," he said, "takes time. And by the time I got back to him he was dead. And it's all my fault."

"No, it isn't," the detective said. "Jeffrey was dead at least two hours by then. All self-administered as far as we can tell. There were no signs of a struggle, except the knife wounds, which he got two hours earlier at Rosalie's house and which weren't even near to being fatal. He'd been close to death twice before, due to heavy addiction to methamphetamines. Lying to law enforcement was always wrong, now it's dumb besides. Doesn't everybody know the police have science working for them now? Don't any of you watch 'CSI'?"

"Oh, well," Fred Berryman said, sniffing, "TV."

With more than two million books printed worldwide, Ms Grei-man currently lives on the Minnesota tundra with her family, some of whom are human. In her spare time she likes to ride some of her more hirsute companions in high speed events such as barrel racing and long distance endurance rides.

Iced

Lois Greiman

"What do you mean you don't have any honey oat rolls?"
Howard T. Crandell stood in the Sandwich Station on Washington Avenue and glared across the counter at the shop's newest employee. Her hair was a shade reminiscent of eggplant, his least favorite fruit. Thirteen piercings punctured strategic parts of her visible anatomy, and the nametag that hung askew on her oversized chest read Alleigh. He might just as well have glared at a parking meter. It would have been equally impressed.

Alleigh with the superfluous letters, however, managed a shrug, making her, perhaps, somewhat more accomplished than an inanimate object.

"Won't be done for another ten minutes or so," she added.

"Or so?" Howard felt his arteries plump up with adrenaline.

She performed another shrug, one surely orchestrated to make his frontal veins burst. "Could be fifteen."

"Fifteen!" Panic was beginning to build. Three beads of sweat popped out on his upper lip despite the below ridiculous temperatures served up by Minnesota in January. "You might as well wait for next Christmas. You might as well wait..." He calmed himself, took a cleansing breath as his psychiatrist had repeatedly recommended, and tried adding a smile. He'd never been particularly adept at smiling. A few members of the female persuasion had suggested it looked maniacal. "Ghoulish" had been mentioned on more than one occasion.

Alleigh took a step back, convincing Howard to abandon the expression. It was nothing if not a relief. "But it's Friday," he said. He always took the early lunch shift on Fridays and it always consisted of a turkey Swiss sandwich on a honey oat roll with just a smidgen of sunny lemon mayo and five spinach leaves.

Sandwich girl was eyeing him warily. This time she didn't quite manage a shrug. The parking meter was looking more proficient by the second.

"Listen..." He wasn't above pleading. "There must be something you can do." He had a meeting with Mr. Midal in twenty-two minutes. Maybe it would be *good* news, he thought, but Midal had met with Howard's supervisor earlier in the day and that didn't necessarily boost his optimism. His gut churned nervously. He couldn't be late for the meeting. It took seven minutes to trudge through the black sludge to the IDS tower where he had a cubicle at Granger and Pope Insurance, two to sharpen his pencils and align them just so, and four to make his way up to the fourteen floor. That left him just nine minutes to spare; in the end he could wait no longer and left the Sandwich Station in defeat.

He stopped at the first shop down on Marquette, and although they clearly did not have the proper type of mayo, his stomach insisted he order something. Eventually, he sat at a plastic corner table with his back to the wall, cut the sandwich in four precise quadrants and tasted his first bite. Due consideration followed. After which, he folded the remainder of the sandwich neatly back in its foil wrapper and discarded it in the proper receptacle. Seventeen minutes still remained before his meeting, but he liked to be seven minutes early to every appointment. Six made him nervous. Eight made him appear neurotic. He didn't like to appear neurotic.

Straightening his bowtie, Howard entered the front door and showed his badge to the security guard. Melvin Odin was big and bald-headed and made his pulse skitter like a toddler on black ice even though Howard was pretty sure he could beat Melvin in a foot race. Melvin's pack-a-day habit was reducing his lung capacity and shortening his life expectancy by two months every calendar year, giving him an 83.7 percent chance of dying before he reached retirement.

After taking care of his daily pencil duties, Howard marched from his cubicle toward the waiting elevator. Margaret Swanson was scowling at her computer screen. She'd been drinking again. From the narrow corridors that ran through the office as if through a rabbit warren, he could smell the breath mints she always used after a hard night at Brit's Pub.

Tommy Olson was on the phone. "Yes, sir," he said into the receiver. He was standing ramrod straight, which he always did when talking to women. His bride, a Valkyrie of five-eleven, made Tommy look like a garden gnome by comparison. Overcompensation, Dr. Tudor would call it.

"Howard." Ralph Midal stepped into the doorway of his office and motioned Howard inside. "Come in. Come in." Mr. Midal was fit and tan and car-commercial handsome. His low BMI and skin pigment was attributed to long hours spent at the Olympic Hills Country Club. His good looks had been inherited from his mother, his money from his dad. But he'd earned his true fortune the old-fashioned way. He'd married it. Greta MacBey Midal was an heiress in her own right. She had once been young, slim, and stunning. Middle-aged now, the only thing about her that was likely to stun was the Tazer she kept in the outside middle pocket of her over-the-shoulder Coach bag. That's why Howard tried to avoid her; he had been known, on more than one occasion, to tell the truth when the truth was not strictly called for. *She* had been known to zap acquaintances for just such an offense.

"You look well," Ralph blustered and patted Howard's arm as he shut the door behind them.

Howard watched the action and felt his gut churn. Ralph Midal left his office door open 97.3 percent of the time, only closing it when firing employees and talking to mistresses.

Howard Crandel was pretty sure they weren't lovers.

"What's going on?" Howard asked and tugged weakly at his tie. He wasn't claustrophobic...exactly...

"Listen, Howard, you know I really like you."

Panic welled up in earnest; noboby *really* liked him. "I'm good at my job," he said, but his voice had already gone squeaky. "I'm the best actuary in the Twin Cities. Well, one of the two best." He winced. "Third best if you count Peter Winters. But he's retired so..." He felt winded. "I'm good at what I do," he finished poorly.

"Yes you are. Of course you are. Have a seat, Howard. Please," Ralph said and motioned an elegant hand toward the plush chair that faced his desk. "You see...that's just the trouble; I'm afraid you're *too* good at your job."

Howard remained standing. "There's no such thing as being

too good at a job."

Ralph chuckled. "Of course there is. I worry that we're holding you back."

"You're not."

Mr. Midal rubbed the back of his neck. His face was a little flushed. "You're always forthright, Howard. *I* like that about you. But..." He tilted his head as if participating in an internal tussle while Howard sprinted through a dozen past scenarios in his mind. Three popped up as particularly note-worth.

"I was just trying to help her," he said.

"Help who?"

"Alicia. It's her third pregnancy in fifty-two months."

Midal shook his head.

"Statistically speaking, one of those children will probably be a high-school drop out. They'll each have a ten percent chance of becoming a pornography addict before the age of seventeen and will also have a forty-two percent probability of using illegal drugs."

For a second Mr. Midal conjured up the same confused expression that had often graced Howard's mother's face, but he shook it off. "Sue thinks you're bad for company morale."

Howard blinked at him. Sue wore a size eight shoe, had an odd penchant for Beanie Babies, and was rarely seen without a metal water bottle filled with Crystal Light. She was also his supervisor. "Susan doesn't like me," he said. It didn't take a mathematical genius to figure that out.

Midal began to shake his head again but paused, curious. "Did you really tell her she was forty pounds overweight?"

"No." Howard tried to hold back the truth, but it was like attempting to redirect a Minnesota blizzard. "I told her she was forty-two point seven pounds overweight."

"Which is the average weight of a..." Midal paused, waiting for Howard to fill in the blanks.

"An Australian Cattle Dog."

For a moment Mr. Midal's face did funny things. It almost looked like he was going to laugh, or cry, or throw up. Sometimes, despite Howard's talents in other areas, he wasn't particularly astute at reading people's facial expressions.

"I thought it might help her," Howard added.

"You did?"

He nodded. "The chances of finding a husband are significantly · lower for women who carry more than twenty-seven percent body fat. Add her advancing years to the equation and she's more likely to become the princess of a third world country than be married again."

"Is that actually true?"

"No, sir," he said. Perspiration had begun to accumulate around the back of his collar. "That was a joke."

"Oh," Midal said. "Well...listen, Howard...I'm afraid I'm going to have to let you go."

The room seemed very quiet suddenly and dangerously airtight. Howard pursed his lips. "I can quit saying things like that."

Midal watched him. "I really don't think you can."

"I can," he said, hopelessly hopeful. "I can quit talking to people all together." It would be no great hardship.

"That's very gallant of you, Howard. And I appreciate the offer. Granger and Pope appreciates the offer. In fact, we're giving you a very attractive severance package so that you can find a job better suited to your unique—"

"I want *this* job," he insisted, but in the end there was nothing he could do. No promises he could make. No arguments that would change his fate. The edict was upheld and effective immediately.

He felt as if every living soul was watching him as he made the walk of shame back to his desk. Every eye was focused on him as he loaded his few belongings into a cardboard box.

There wasn't much to take. Most of the sparse, neatly aligned items on his desktop belonged to Granger and Pope. But he took the stapler. The heavy duty EZ Squeeze 400 had cost him sixty-three dollars and ninety-nine cents and could fasten fifty-five pages together at once.

After that there was nothing for him to do but leave. His head felt empty, his gut the same. He blinked as he stepped into the brittle winter sunlight. So the world hadn't stopped. His stomach rumbled. He wandered unsteadily toward the Sandwich Station. But then he saw her. Susan Amelia Peterson. The woman who had cost him his job. She was swinging her oversized hand bag and laughing flirtatiously with Greg Nordell from accounting. Anger, or something like it, sluiced through him. He turned in a haze and marched across Nicollet to confront her.

She tossed her hair off her neck as he stalked toward her. Greg leaned in, probably slipping in another famous one-liner. The accountants were the lady's men at Granger and Pope.

Sue draped her fingers in front of her neck, smoothing them downward in a provocative fashion. By the time Howard mounted the opposite curb, she was laughing again. But her humor sounded like a witch's cackle to his ears. She turned toward him. Her eyes widened in fear. Well, she should be afraid. He hadn't deserved to be fired.

"I bet you thought I'd take this lying down," he said.

She croaked something at him.

"Well, I'm not going to. I'm going to...to...write a letter to—"

"Pen!" she rasped and clawed at her purse.

Greg Nordell had backed off a couple of steps and was staring at her with uncertain eyes.

Howard glared. "I've got my own pen. Thank you very much."

"Pen!" she gasped again. Her eyes were wide and bloodshot.

"Have you been drinking?" Howard asked.

That's when her purse toppled to the sidewalk. She dropped to all fours beside it.

Howard glanced down in surprise and distaste. "Mr. Midal doesn't like it when-"

"Please—" She looked up at him, hand on her throat, eyes bulging.

"Your face is awful red."

"Epi—"

"You're not supposed to imbibe during business hours."

Pedestrians were beginning to murmur around them.

"Need—" she rasped and fell with a plop onto Howard's neatly polished right shoe.

He stared down at her, perplexed and a little disgruntled.

Gasps and whispers sighed around him.

"...some sort of reaction!"

Those were the words that ripped him from his stupor. Reaction! Lunch! Allergies!

"Peanuts!" he squawked and yanked his foot out from under

her heaving body. "Help! Ambulance! Help!"

"What's happening?" Greg was gripping Howard's coat sleeve with spastic fingers, but Howard didn't have the wherewithal to remember he hated to be touched.

"Peanuts! Allergic reaction!"

"What? She didn't have any-"

"911," he yelled.

A dozen people snapped open cell phones.

"But she didn't have any nuts," Greg insisted.

She was lying on her side now, gasping, eyes protruding.

"Epi—" she said again. That was when the gong went off in Howard's jam-packed brain.

Epinephrine! Snatching her huge bag from beside her prone body, he yanked it open and skimmed the contents. Tattered tissues and scraps of ambiguous notes seemed to float like confetti in front of his eyes.

For a moment, he was tempted almost beyond control to scold her for her messiness, but her lips were turning purple.

He snapped his attention back to the purse and dipped his hand inside. Three tampons, five cheap pens, and two Tootsie Pops came away in his fingers.

"I don't think it's here," he rasped.

That's when Greg grabbed the purse from him and dumped the contents onto the sidewalk. Her water bottle rolled toward the street while a half dozen other items skittered off in every direction. "What does it look like?" he snapped.

Howard glanced at the tumbled contents then, "Here!" he yelled and snatched up the device filled with epinephrine. But what now? He turned it over. Directions were on the back.

"Flip open the top." He read the words aloud, but suddenly a commanding voice boomed through the open air mall.

"Get back!" The crowd parted like the Red Sea. Ralph Midal charged through and towered over them. "My God! Sue, what happened?"

She croaked a response. His eyes widened. He shot his gaze to Howard, snatched the pen from his hand and in one smooth move, stabbed it into the woman's thigh.

There were gasps, oohs, and hopeful whisperings, but two

minutes later Susan Amelia Peterson was dead.

"Is that correct, Mr. Crandell." Detective Greenberg was tall, muscular and intimidating. She had a body fat percentage of approximately 9.3; Detective Greenberg might live forever.

"What?" He glanced up, feeling fuzzy and off-kilter even though he was in his own little house on Ewing Avenue.

"You were just fired today?"

He blinked, nodded, wondered if the Sandwich Station had honey oat rolls yet.

"And Susan Peterson...she was your supervisor?"

"What?"

She repeated the question.

"Oh, yes, that's correct."

"Tell me, Mr. Crandell, were you aware that Ms Peterson was allergic to peanuts?"

"Yes."

"And you were familiar with the fact that she often went to the Hub for lunch?"

"Every Monday and Friday. She liked their hot fudge cake even though she always was trying to lose... " He stopped, glanced up, blinked. "You don't think I had anything to do with..."

She was staring at him.

"With..." He shook his head, bumbled to his feet. No honey oat rolls for lunch and now this! "I wouldn't kill her."

"How long have you been with Granger and Pope, Mr. Crandell?"

"Seven years, two months and seventeen days, but..."

"You must have really enjoyed your job there if you know to the day how long you've been in their employ."

He scowled. "I also know I've been talking to you for twenty-four minutes and thirteen seconds and I don't like—" He stopped himself...again. This was unprecedented self control.

She stared at him. Her dark hair was pulled back in a no-nonsense ponytail, showcasing her strong features, her steady eyes. One brow was raised.

He swallowed. "I didn't kill her," he said.

"But you were angry."

Had he been? He wasn't very familiar with emotion. Certainly wasn't comfortable with it. "She died. She just died. She had an anaphylactic reaction. Legumes are extremely allergenic. There are three point three million people with similar allergies. Forty-three percent..." He paused.

She stared at him.

"I didn't kill her," he repeated. Some of the steam had gone out of his sails.

"The employees at the Hub say the same thing. They swear there were no peanuts served to her."

"Maybe they used peanut oil. Peanut oil—"

"According to the *sous* chef they only use extra virgin olive oil."

"Well, I didn't kill her."

"Duly noted," she said and flipped her notebook shut. "Just stick around." She was already headed toward the door.

He followed her. "Why? Why should I stick around?"

She turned toward him, expression deadpan. "Who else are we going to ask if we want to know how many seconds it takes to get from your kitchen to your bathroom?"

He didn't sleep well that night even though he drank five ounces of warm milk, put on his white noise maker, and did fifteen minutes of stretches before turning out the lights. Something niggled at his mind.

At 5:36 AM he sat bolt upright in his bed. At 5:37 he called Detective Greenberg's cell phone.

"Hello?"

"Where's her canteen?" His voice sounded gritty to his own ears. He usually began the day with a half a teaspoon of salt dissolved in fourteen ounces of tepid bottled water. "She always has a canteen."

He could hear her yawn, shift, rustle the bedsprings as if glancing at the clock. But there were no murmurs of protest from a partner. Detective Greenberg slept alone.

"Her canteen," he repeated. "One of those metal bottles that's supposed to be environmentally friendly but spreads bacteria like the black death and—" he paused. "She liked to drink Crystal

Light. Thought it helped her control her appetite even though her weight..." He stopped again. "It was in her purse when Greg dumped it onto the sidewalk. Maybe there was something in *there* that caused her death."

"Mr. Crandell?"

"Yes?"

"Are you aware what time it is?"

"It's 5:37." He glanced at his watch. "Sorry, 5:38...and twenty-two seconds. Twenty-*three* seconds. Why?"

She sighed. "I'll call you later," she said and hung up.

The next twelve hours passed miserably. Howard ate, prepared a bag lunch for a job he no longer had, spoke to Detective Green-berg, vacuumed twice, and straightened the stapler that sat in the middle of his modest dining room table. At 5:17 PM the phone rang. He answered, blinked, and spoke. A half an hour later, he opened the door for Mr. Midal. It had already been dark for twenty-three minutes. January in Minnesota barely saw the light of day.

"Howard," Mr. Midal said and shook his head. He was dressed in a dark cashmere coat and leather gloves. "Thank you so much for seeing me."

"Sure," Howard said and remained where he was. They stared at each other.

"May I come in?" Midal asked.

"Oh. Yes," Howard said and stepped aside.

Midal walked in and glanced around. "You have a nice place here. Nice and... orderly."

"I like to keep things...sterile. Did they find Susan's canteen?"

"That's what I came to talk to you about."

Howard fidgeted. "Her water bottle?"

"Sue," Midal corrected and smiled grimly. "She was an excellent employee."

"No, she—" Howard began but he stopped himself. It was wrong to speak poorly of the dead. "Sure," he said. It was hard to push the words past his teeth, but he managed it. A half a decade of psychiatric intervention had not been in vain. "Sure she was."

"It's going to be hard without her."

"Couldn't Kent do her job?" *Or just about anyone else?* He didn't add that. Dr. Tudor would be proud.

Mr. Midal sighed, shook his head, and looked extremely sad. "It's an awful situation. Just awful. But the short of it is, Howard, I want you to come back."

"Me?" He couldn't have been more surprised if Midal had said he wanted to hire a leprechaun to do the bookkeeping.

"It would mean a substantial raise for you."

"I just... But you fired me. You said I was bad for morale."

"That's what Sue said, but..." He grinned. "Well, maybe we need to shake things up a little. And with you as supervisor, Granger and Pope just might be able to—"

"Supervisor!" Howard took a rapid step to the rear. "That would mean I would have to... I would have to talk to people all the time."

Midal laughed now. Mr. jolly. "Well, we would try to keep that to a minimum. The important thing is that we get you back in the office."

Howard winced. "Would I have to have lunch with people, too?"

"We can worry about that when the time comes. Just tell me you'll accept my offer."

"Would I have to—"

Impatience ticked in the older man's jaw. Howard was not a stranger to that tic. "You can keep your old job if you want to."

"Oh." His heart felt a little better. "Okay."

"The thing is, it's time to put Sue's death behind us."

"But they haven't even figured out who killed—" he began, but Mr. Midal interrupted him.

"She died of an allergic reaction, Howard. Everyone knows that. It's a terrible tragedy. No one mourns her loss more than I do. She and Greta were personal friends."

"You mean...she didn't tell your wife about your mistress?"

For just a second, Midal's jaw dropped, but he pulled himself together in an instant. "I don't know what you're talking about."

Howard scowled. "The woman who picked you up at the corner of 5th and Hennepin last Tuesday. The one with the dark hair and the big—"

"You must be talking about my cousin, Sarah."

Howard scowled. "*My* cousin never kisses me on the lips." Of course, his cousin wore a full beard and liked to be called Scratch.

"Sarah—" Midal began then drew a deep breath and pressed a tight smile onto his face. "I'll never hold it against you that you have an over-active imagination, Howard."

"I don't have an imagination at—"Howard began, but Ralph held up his hand.

"Do you want the job or not?"

"Yes. Yes, of course. Of course, I want the job."

"Then for the sake of the company...for the sake of all our employees, we must move on. Can you do that, Howard?"

"Move on?"

"Forget about Sue's death."

"I suppose so. I just wonder where her canteen—" He paused, thought, tilted his head. "Weren't you in her office yesterday morning?"

For a moment Mr. Midal stood entirely motionless then he laughed. "She was a supervisor, Howard. I went into her office on quite a regular basis."

"Yes, I suppose..." He scowled. "But you were carrying something."

He shrugged. "I don't think so."

"You were. You were—"

"Okay, I don't know why it matters, but perhaps I was carrying the Truman file."

"In your pocket."

"What?"

"There was something in your pocket."

"My cell phone, I suppose. See? I have it here right now," he said and pulled it out of his trousers pocket.

Howard nodded. "Sure," he said. "Sure, but you had something in your jacket pocket, too."

"Listen, Howard, you're a good actuary. That's why I've put up with your eccentricities. But I'm getting rather tired of—"

"Inside," he said. "On the left side. I know because your coat hung a little bit off kilter, and there was a tiny divet in the fabric.

Your suits are always tailored so well. They usually hang perfectly straight."

"Who knew you were a fashionista?"

Howard shrugged. His stomach churned. "Who knew you were a murderer?"

Mr. Midal's face went cold. "What are you talking about?"

Howard felt sick to his stomach. "Susan was blackmailing you, wasn't she, Mr. Midal?"

"Are you on medication?"

"I wasn't the only one who knew you were having an affair."

Mr. Midal's face was flushed. "You don't want to do this, Howard."

"That's why she got the promotion instead of Kent."

"I'm offering you your job back."

"Your wife would divorce you if she found out."

"There was nothing to find out."

"You knew Sue had peanut allergies. You had access to her canteen. You put peanut oil in her Crystal Light."

Midal laughed. It had excellent pitch. "You can't honestly think I poisoned her?"

"I can't argue with facts."

"That's ridiculous. Everyone knows she carries epinephrine with her. I was the one who administered it to her. I was the one who tried to save her life, for God's sake."

"They can't find the EpiPen."

"It was lost in the crowd."

"It *and* her canteen? The odds are astronomical. No." He shook his head. "You got rid of them," Howard said. "Because you'd tampered with them. The EpiPen is supposed to be a tamper-proof syringe, but you're an intelligent man and you had a fortune to protect. My guess is you bought a device just like hers, filled it with saline then somehow—"

Midal's hand moved so fast it was little more than a blur, but when he paused, Howard blinked.

"Oh," he said. "You've got a gun. I...I... Funny I didn't see *that* in your pocket."

Mr. Midal took a step toward him. Howard stepped back.

"A gun," Howard repeated.

"I didn't want it to come to this," Midal said.

"What is that?" Sweat had already saturated his carefully buttoned shirt collar. "A nine millimeter Beretta?" he asked and bumped off his perfectly aligned bookshelves.

"I don't know why you couldn't leave well enough alone."

"I'm told those Barettas are very loud." He raised his voice when he said it.

"I was willing to give you your job back even though you're the most irritating man—"

"And it'll get blood..." He backed into a dining room chair, straightened it, backed around it. "It'll get blood on my carpet."

"Good bye" Ralph said and raised the pistol.

Howard reached frantically behind him. The heavy duty EZ Squeeze 400 came away in his fingers. He threw it for all he was worth. It richocheted off Midal's wrist. Howard bolted into the kitchen.

In that second, the front door slammed open.

"Put the gun down!"

Midal's footfalls slowed to a halt. Howard dashed into the kitchen, ducked, then peeked out from behind a kitchen chair.

Detective Greenberg stood in the doorway, thighs flexed, arms outstretched.

"Put it down!" she barked.

Midal turned, Beretta in hand, but two officers were flanking her. He tilted the muzzle toward the ceiling.

"Mother of God!" Howard squawked and stepped tentatively into the living room. "What took you so long?"

"It's twenty degrees below zero," Greenberg said, not taking her gaze from Midal, not fiddling with the hearing device in her right ear. "Sometimes the cold makes reception kind of iffy."

"Iffy..." Howard staggered back a step and slid down the living room wall to the floor. "...maybe that would have been good information to share."

"Read him his rights," Greenberg said, nodding to the cops behind her. Two of them rushed forward.

"In the future," Howard said hazily, "Perhaps you should not suggest that civilians goad the perpetrator into a confession unless the outside temperature exceeds the minimum required for good reception."

She grinned a little, cracking dimples into her cheeks as she lowered her gun. "What's the problem, Crandell? Everything turned out all right."

"What's the problem? What's the...He tried to kill me," he said, motioning weakly toward where two officers were handcuffing Mr. Midal. "Did you notice that he tried to kill me?"

She offered him her hand. Her balance was as steady as a rock as she helped him to his feet. "But he didn't succeed. And now you can get on with your life."

"What are you talking about?"

She shrugged. "Move on. Start a new career. With a mind like yours you could make a pretty decent P.I."

He snorted. "A private investigator?"

"Why not?" she asked. "They only make about sixty percent as much as actuaries do, but they're one hundred percent more likely to get a girlfriend."

"Really?" he asked and tried another smile. It might have still looked maniacal but it felt a little less ghoulish.

Pat Dennis is the author of *Hotdish To Die For*, a collection of culinary mystery short stories where the weapon of choice is often hotdish. Her fiction and humor have been published in *Minnesota Monthly*, *Woman's World*, *The Pioneer Press* and other publications. She is the editor and a contributor to the anthology of mystery short stories of crimes and bathrooms entitled *Who Died In Here?* Pat works as a stand-up comedian for special events and is married to an air traffic controller who goes to work to get away from the stress.

Minnesota Iced

Pat Dennis

"No way," Adeline sputtered, her thick fingers grasping her cup of St John's Wort herbal tea tightly. Even the crackling noises emitting from antique woodstove in the far corner of the room couldn't cheer her up. Nothing could. Not as long as her mother-in-law was planning to visit.

"Way," her husband replied, his horn-rimmed glasses resting on the tip of his fleshy, bulbous nose. He brushed back his stringy, thin hair with his spindly hand before folding the Sunday paper carefully into quarters.

"Really, Karl? Your mother wants to spend the rest of the winter with us?" Adeline asked before shaking back her salt and pepper hair in frustration. She could feel her anxiety grow minute by minute. Her puffy hand reached for a chocolate butter cream that rested in the opened candy box in the middle of their red Formica table, but she pulled her arm back quickly. If she wanted to be under two-seventy by New Year's Eve, she'd have to limit her daily intake of Russell Stover.

Karl peered over his glasses. "She told me she wants to spend every single winter from now on, as well," he stated flatly, as if the news he shared was little more than a passing comment about the weather and not marital Armageddon.

Adeline pouted in silence, but she knew she didn't have to remain silent. She could say almost anything about the vile witch and her husband wouldn't mind. He never disagreed with her, not even when she yammered on about his nasty mother. Being the son of four-time divorcee Dorothy Nordskov hadn't been easy for him. It was no wonder to Adeline that he'd been married as many times, himself. But she was determined to make their marriage be the one that counted in his life. It certainly did for Adeline. Karl was the first man who'd ever given a flying fig about her.

She crossed her arms and rested them on top of her ample chest "I thought old people hated the cold."

"We're old and we love living in Minnesota," he reminded her.

"We're barely in our 60s. She's like a gazillion or something."

"Eighty-eight years of age and still going strong," her husband bragged.

Too strong, Adeline pined. That woman should have died years ago from cheap booze, unfiltered cigarettes, and a string of bitter, gun-toting ex-husbands. Though she'd only known her for a few years, as far as Adeline was concerned the woman was past her expiration date.

"Can't we just send her a letter asking her not to come?" Adeline suggested, her voice turning to sultry molasses. There was no way she'd telephone the dilapidated fartress. Even the sound of her gin-slurred voice made Adeline's Scandinavian skin crawl.

The first time she'd met Dorothy was at their wedding. The woman hadn't bothered to bring them either a present or offer to chip in on their lavish, three-course reception held at the American Legion Hall. Instead, her mother-in-law insisted that Karl pay her for airline ticket, stating that she'd been to one too many of her son's weddings to shell out another thin dime.

If that wasn't bad enough, Adeline overheard her mother-in-law calling her gullible. That comment hurt her feelings, but not any more than the fact that her newly wedded husband didn't have the backbone to stand up for her. No telling how their relationship would deteriorate if Dorothy were to live with them. The two of them would be snickering behind Adeline's back the minute she turned around to flip a Weight Watcher's pancake.

"Did *you* forget it's her cabin?" her husband asked while focusing on the crossword puzzle in front of him. He removed the thin pencil from behind his ear and began to fill in the nine-letter answer for the meaning of *Santa's staff* — c-a-n-d-y c-a-n-e.

Adeline asked, "Did *you* forget she left you this cabin in her will?"

Karl didn't bother to look up. "A will kicks in after someone dies, not before."

"That doesn't seem fair. I mean, technically it's your place."

Adeline insisted.

"Technically it is, when she's dead. Let it go, Adeline. There's nothing we can do to stop her from coming. She'll be here by noon tomorrow."

"But we're still on our honeymoon," Adeline whined. True, they'd been married for a few years, but to Adeline they were still as happy as newlyweds. In fact, though they slept in separate bedrooms due to her snoring, they were still having sex every other month.

Adeline was 61 when she'd met Karl through an online forum for puzzle aficionados. Although she was mainly interested in simple themes like Hollywood celebrities or TV trivia, Karl's passion for being a cruciverbalist won her heart. He'd spend an entire day working a single New York Times crossword. So, it was easy for her to understand why it had been too difficult for him to ever hold a real job for very long.

Karl took a long sip of his Irish coffee before trying to comfort her. He said, "Don't worry, dear. My mother will die soon."

Not soon enough, Adeline thought to herself. She wouldn't make it to spring herself if she had to share a cabin with her mother-in-law. It was obvious. One of them would be forced to leave the cabin, one way or another.

The following morning, Adeline was up at five a.m., the same time she awoke every morning. But this time, Adeline's eyes opened with a purpose. She had only a few hours to prepare the ice-fishing shanty for her mother-in-law's accident.

But first, Adeline had to do what needed to be done every morning. Living in the isolated northland in winter wasn't easy. There was wood to be chopped, paths to be shoveled, coffee to be ground by hand, and a full English breakfast to be made. More importantly, her work needed to be accomplished without disturbing her sleeping giant of a husband.

Poor Karl. If she weren't careful, she'd wake him as she crept by his closed bedroom door. If she did disturb him, he'd stumble out of his room, insisting through a big yawn that he felt well enough to help with her daily chores. Even when his back was killing him, he'd never uttered a word of complaint. Instead, he would bravely place his hand behind him to support his weakening spine.

"Arthritis," he'd explained on their first real date. "I'm afraid you can't expect me to be of much help."

But Karl's inability to pitch in didn't usually bother Adeline. She'd watched her own mother cater to her father's needs until her mom finally died from exhaustion. It was no wonder to her that father's grief led him to do crazy things—like move to Phoenix and marry a web-cam stripper.

What did surprise her, however, was that Karl owned a cabin and his own private lake. Never once in her life did she allow herself to dream of spending even one night in such luxury, much less becoming the owner's wife. For the first time in her life, her home wasn't a dingy, poorly furnished apartment with a tiny window that overlooked a cat-filled alley.

Now, her view out of the cabin's kitchen large frost-filled window was picture postcard perfect. Adeline adored their small lake which was usually frozen thick with ice by mid-November. Surrounding the shoreline were a hundred towering tamaracks whose branches were bent downward from the weight of wet snow. A portable ice fishing shack sat smack dab in the middle of their artic-like oasis. Now that she was retired, she could ice fish all afternoon if she wanted.

The landscape was so serene she could almost see the silence hovering in mid-air. In fact, the nearest neighbors were two lakes over. This northern paradise had belonged in the Nordokov family for generations, its title held onto with a deathlike grip through multiple divorces or descendants' untimely deaths. Now, through a quirk of fate and community property it belonged to Adeline as well.

No one was going to ruin it for her. No one.

Adeline filled the glass coffee pot with cold water and slipped it back into its cradle. She set the machine's timer to start brewing in four hours. Karl should be up by then. She would have preferred to have a cup right now to kick start her day, but she knew her husband would never drink reheated coffee. He was classy that way.

Besides, it seemed like such a little thing to do for him, considering all that he did for her. Not only did he provide a lakefront home, but also almost weekly he'd go online to order little gifts for her. Every few days a box of mixed nuts or rich confections would arrive via the post. And Karl never went into town without bringing back a gallon of pistachio ice cream and a family size bucket of Kentucky Fried Chicken for her to enjoy. Adeline had managed to gain an additional 80 pounds since she said first uttered the words, *I do*. If she didn't know any better, she'd have thought Karl was trying to kill her with kindness.

Adeline reached over to the oak coat rack that held her winter gear. She grabbed her worn, silver down jacket that was repaired with strands of duct tape and slipped it on. She sat down on a chair in order to pull on her scruffy winter boots. But she halted her efforts, choosing to stare instead at the puddle of water and snow that had gathered on the floor in the front of her.

"What the..." she said to herself and then looked upwards at the ceiling. She didn't notice any leaks or watermarks. In fact when she lowered her sight and followed the trail of slush with her eyes, it seemed to end right outside of her husband's bedroom door.

She wondered briefly if Karl had been up during the middle of the night to venture outdoors. Perhaps he couldn't sleep and went for a midnight stroll, though that seemed unlikely. He'd never done anything like that before. Still, her mother always told her to never be surprised by an aging husband's actions. All men acted a little odder as they grew older.

Adeline decided to wait to clean up the mess. Her time was running out. She tied her boots and tossed a long, black wool scarf around her neck a couple of times. She yanked her hand-knitted orange cap down around her ears and opened the door to step out into the bitter cold.

She began shoveling a clear route to the shanty. Normally, she wouldn't have bothered to do so. She'd just use her extra wide feet to trample flat a pathway to her favorite spot. She was the only one who visited the tiny house. Sitting in a poorly heated, plastic shanty while waiting for a fish to bite was something her husband had no interest in doing.

Fortunately, Adeline remembered that her mother-in-law claimed to adore ice fishing as a young girl. With any luck, Adeline would be able to convince her to try it one more time. Adeline would help navigate the fragile woman across the slippery surface, and then once inside the hut she'd accidentally brush into her mother-in-law, causing the boozed-up senior citizen to tumble into the soon-to-be enlarged hole in the center of the floor.

Of course the opening wouldn't be big enough for Dorothy to disappear into completely. But, it would be large enough to accommodate a good portion of her lower extremities. The hyperthermia that would follow could easily kill the inebriated elder within a matter of minutes, especially if Adeline took her time walking back to the cabin for help. She'd even call 911 before waking her husband to tell him of the terrible incident that had just occurred. Adeline knew if she timed it right, he'd be in bed at 2 p.m., like he was everyday. Karl loved nothing better than a pleasant, daily siesta.

Of course, if being dipped in frigid water didn't manage to end her mother-in-law's life, it would certainly help to bring on a bout of deadly pneumonia. Adeline assumed the octogenarian had few, if any rebounds left in her. If being soaked didn't do it to her, Adeline would help her mother-in-law recuperate by serving her sandwiches made from raw poultry or undercooked pork. Perhaps Adeline could even whip up a cream of Liberty Cap mushroom soup. She had comprised a list of two-dozen ways she could ensure her mother-in-law's hasty passage into the beyond.

Thank god for Google, Adeline mused as she breathed in a blast of cold air.

She'd only shoveled another minute or so when the sound of her husband's voice surprised her. She swirled around to see him standing in the cabin doorway, fully dressed in layers of flannel and denim. Even his leathers boots were laced up tight.

His hands were shoved deep inside his pockets when he asked, "Why are you shoveling so early? It isn't even light out."

Adeline didn't bother to tell him she always shoveled in the wee hours of the morning, for fear of waking him. Instead she asked, "What are you doing up? Did I wake you when I walked by your room?"

She hadn't noticed any light protruding from underneath his doorway. But, if she had, Adeline would have assumed he'd fallen asleep while doing another one of his puzzles.

He shook his head and said, "Nah, I've been awake for hours.

I even went for a walk. I wanted to get everything done I promised my mom I'd do before she arrives."

She wanted to retort, *Like what? Remove the little bit of backbone you have left?* Instead she said, "Go back to bed. I can do everything. Once I finish shoveling, I'll start on the laundry and carry in some wood."

A look of concern crossed his face. He asked, "Will you have time to make the Tater Tot hot dish she likes?"

Adeline wanted to point out that time wouldn't be an issue, if he could help out just a bit. But, she knew it was important that he always thought of her as a good and obedient wife. She needed him on her side if the police decided to investigate her mother-in-law's unfortunate accident. She said, "Don't worry. I'll make time."

Karl used his finger to point at the tool that stuck out of her jacket. With a stern face he asked, "What's that?"

Adeline hesitated for a moment, trying to formulate a quick response. Normally Karl didn't give a rat's behind about her fishing habits. She shrugged her shoulders, as if it were no big deal. She said, "It was so cold last night, I figured the fishing hole in the shack is probably covered over with new ice." She pulled the chisel out of her pocket and held it in the air. "I decided it would be easier to chip through it, rather than use the auger."

Of course she'd used the hand held auger she kept in the corner of her shanty, as well. But, she didn't tell Karl that. Her husband didn't need to know that she was planning to double the size of the 12" inch access to the deadly water that flowed beneath the ice.

Surprisingly, he shot her a flirtatious wink and announced, "I left you something in the shanty. It's a little gift that arrived yesterday in the mail."

"Candy?" she asked, realizing that the real reason Karl had went outside in the middle of the night. He wanted to surprise her. *Could there be a sweeter man?* She wondered.

"Maybe," he shrugged. "Just keep shoveling and you'll find the little secret my mom and I planned for you."

Adeline gulped. Her mother-in-law was in on the surprise? Maybe Dorothy wasn't as bad as she thought. Maybe she shouldn't actually go through with her plan to be rid of her once and for all.

She'd actually thought about killing her mother-in-law from

the first day she met her. But, she'd never gone through with it. Maybe she shouldn't this time either. Maybe she wouldn't even bring Dorothy to her ice fishing shack. The shanty was, after all, Adeline's special place to get away from the world. Maybe she shouldn't tarnish it with murder.

Adeline began to shovel furiously toward her surprise, tossing piles of snow on either side of her. Though she was a few years older than Karl, he always made her feel like a giddy teenager. She could feel Karl's eyes still on her, watching her. She wondered if the sight of her ample rump moving with every stroke turned him on? She'd heard that some men were weird that way.

She decided to treat him to a bit of wiggling while she continued her effort. She made it to just outside of the shanty's door, when she heard a loud crack. And then—another. She saw that the snow beneath her feet had already been removed. She could see large cracks in the ice branching out like a spider web underneath her clearance-priced Eddie Bauer footwear. Out of the corner of her eye, she caught a glimpse of a sledgehammer, than leaned against the Shanty's wall just as the ice below her shattered. She quickly disappeared downward into the black, watery hole.

Her orange hat bobbed up to the surface two more times, until it disappeared from Karl's sight. Adeline was already dead by the time her husband shut the cabin door and dialed 911, slowly.

"I'm surprised she lasted as long as she did," Dorothy said later that day, over a steaming cup of hot chocolate her son had lovingly prepared for her.

"Me, too. With her health the way it was, being a diabetic and a heart patient, I was surprised I could even get a life insurance policy on her," Karl said, as he dropped a half-a-dozen miniature marshmallows into his cup. He added, "I doubt if there will be a need for an autopsy."

"Are you worried about that? She died from an accident. It's not as if you held her head under water," his mother reassured him.

Karl shrugged, "And the ice was bound to crack someday under all the extra weight she was carrying."

"She kept gaining weight until the day she died," his mother reminded him. "She would have died eventually. I'm afraid, we all do."

Karl looked adoringly at his loving mother and for the first time ever he wondered what his life would be like without her. He begged, "Promise me, Mother, that you'll never die."

Dorothy reached over and placed her hand on her Karl's shoulder. She squeezed it gently and whispered, "Don't worry, Son. Like I've always said, I won't let myself die before you do."

Before he became a mystery writer and reviewer, Carl Brookins was a counselor and faculty member at Metropolitan State University in Saint Paul, Minnesota. He has reviewed mystery fiction for the *Saint Paul Pioneer Press* and for *Mystery Scene Magazine*. His reviews now appear on his own web site, on more than a dozen blogs and on several Internet review sites. Brookins is an avid recreational sailor and has sailed in many locations around the world. He is a member of Sisters in Crime, and Private Eye Writers of America. He can frequently be found touring bookstores and libraries with his companions-in-crime, The Minnesota Crime Wave. He writes the sailing adventure series featuring Michael Tanner and Mary Whitney, the Sean Sean private investigator detective series, and the Jack Marston academic mystery series. He lives with his wife of many years, Jean, in Roseville, Minnesota.

www.CarlBrookins.com

The Horse He Rode In On

Carl Brookins

I hate horses. More accurately, I hate riding horseback. Big dumb brutes that only do your bidding when they feel like it. Usually that's never. And they can pretty much throw their weight around whenever they want.

I don't *really* hate horses. They can't help what they are and how they act any more than can a lot of other creatures on this earth. Unlike humans.

I'm perhaps a little sensitive about the weight thing and the size thing because I'm small. I'm five foot two on a good day. I weigh no more'n 130. Naked. Sometimes I throw my weight around, but not as effectively as the horse I was riding this day. A roan mare, Catherine told me. I understand mare. Not roan. Except for size and occasional odd coloring all horses look pretty much alike to me. I suspect it's the same for most folks who don't spend time around horses. Catherine weighs more than me, and she's more'n six feet high. People sometimes snicker when they see us walking hand in hand down a Minneapolis street. Not in Saint Paul. I don't know why people of Saint Paul don't snicker. Maybe they're more polite than the folks in Minneapolis.

We were riding the trails, Catherine and I, in the fields and forests of Horse Heaven Stables, a big ranch south of the Twin Cities. A couple hundred acres of hills, trees and meadows. Maybe a thousand acres. Being from the city, I understand blocks, not acres.

It was a nice, quiet, summer day, not too hot, almost breeze free. I live in a tiny grove of pine trees in an ordinary northern suburb of the Twin Cities. With curbs and a paved road not thirty feet in front of my door. But riding out on a horse, over trails and through the woods, though not to Grandma's house, wasn't my idea of fun.

So why, you might ask, is the consummate urban, short, private detective named Sean NMI Sean engaged in this ridiculous enterprise, something Fang Muhlheisen certainly wouldn't have agreed to. I'm out here astride this beast, following the rural trails of this property because a few days ago, on another nice day, one of the horses on this dude ranch came back from what they call a trail ride here 'bouts, lugging a dead passenger. Councilman Tom Springfield was dead, all right. It was yet to be determined whether it was fortunate or unfortunate that the horse he was on was so gentle that Springfield hadn't fallen off, or been nudged off, all the way back to the barn.

First it was assumed the guy had suffered a heart attack. Accidental death. Case closed. Man was in his late fifties, good health, didn't smoke, et cetera. That still might have been all there was to it except for one curious element.

The horse. The horse he was found slumped astride beside the corral fence next to the barn, was not the horse he rode off on. The medical examiner was alerted. He discovered a contusion on the top of Mr. Springfield's head, concealed by his thick silver hair. The local police decided that the death was suspicious. Where and how had he changed horses? From whence came the dent in his head? Contact with the ground if he fell off the horse? No evidence of that and who put him on a different horse?

Catherine's friends, the Barres, asked me to look into the facts of the matter independently, after the local law began to look hard at the Barres.

"Tell me again why the cops are suspicious of Toni and Dick," I said to Catherine's fine straight back. She made riding a horse look easy, like it was second nature.

"Councilman Springfield was attempting to wrest some or all of this beautiful open land away from the Barres for development."

"Ah," I said, easing myself in the too-wide western style saddle under my bottom. I couldn't ease the chafing too much because this particular saddle, designed for a bigger man than me, podner, had stirrups shortened as much as possible to accommodate Tiny Tim, meaning myself. I'd overheard the stable guy, I think they called him a wrangler, talking to another guy called a swamper. He leaned on a pitchfork watching and chewing, while the first guy shortened the stirrups for me. Standing up in the stirrups was not an option. It gained me, maybe a half inch. Furthermore, the boots I was wearing, not mine own, were grinding on my ankles. I wear perfectly reasonable shoes, red canvas Keds with white soles. But they have no heels. One must have heels to ride astride, keep feet in stirrups. So, borrowed boots and a borrowed western-style hat. No holster or six-shooter. Probably a good thing. In the throes of my rising irritation I might have shot myself.

"The power of eminent domain, eh?" I said. "Take from the few to feather the nests of the many. Especially in the name of community progress." I muttered, just loudly enough to be heard by my companion.

"Apparently so. Over past weeks, the exchanges between Councilman Springfield and Dick and Toni, have become quite acrimonious," Catherine said.

"Yeah, I'll tell ya, Billy, ya let bob wire out here on the range, the neighborhood plumb goes t' hell in a New York minute. Any supporters for the Barres?"

"A few. The folks in town supporting Mr. Springfield seem to be the most vocal."

"You sure we're on the same trail the dead guy took?"

"Quite sure. Toni drew me a map." She waved a scrap of paper at me. Horse pricked up its ears and tossed its head. Danced a few steps to the side. Apparently horses are skittish about fluttering white pieces of paper. Lord only knew what might happen if a dove or an eagle were to happen by.

"Do they make a practice of letting people ride around here on their own?"

"The horse wrangler said I was experienced enough to take care of a bumpkin like you. The councilman insisted he needed to ride out right then and alone. No one was available to go with him and Mr. Springfield was an experienced rider."

"Did he ride out here often?"

"You'll have to ask Toni about that."

"I shall." Toni Barre was a willowy blond who co-owned the stable with her husband. She and Catherine could look each other straight in the eyes. Toni Barre was noticeably fetching in her fawn-colored Stetson, fitted western-style shirt and skin-tight jeans and boots. We sauntered down a gentle slope toward a copse of oak or aspen or maybe walnut trees. I didn't know. Little puffs of dust emanated from the hooves of our mounts on the dry ground. The trail narrowed to single horse-file and my ride, Sally by name, got her nose right over the rump of Catherine's horse which caused the other animal to shy just a little. I pulled back on the reins which Sally seemed to largely ignore, although a little space of separation grew between the animals. A moment later, Sally had eased forward and was again starting to crowd the lead horse. Neither Catherine nor her mount liked it. She glanced back at me and frowned. "Pull her in a little, will you please?"

I did, but holding the animal back put a strain on my arms and shoulders. If I had to do that very long, whatever comfort the ride might have offered would be gone. And why was the horse doing that, anyway? Sally farted. I looked behind me to see her lifting her tail, preparing to make a deposit on the path.

Ordinarily the detective in me might worry about traversing the same trail the dead guy and possibly his assailant had taken. But there weren't that many trails to the scene of the crime. It hadn't rained for days and I saw immediately upon starting along the trail the ground was so dry and loose the least breeze shifted the soil about. Tracking, my Native American acquaintance would have assured me, would be no cakewalk under these conditions.

We went on at a sedate walk. On that I insisted. Eventually the trail widened again and my horse moved up until her nose was a couple of inches ahead of Catherine's horse. That seemed to satisfy her and we rode on in the afternoon. The sun was far abeam on my right. Abeam, that's a sailor's term. I don't know where I learned it. Catherine and her horse were on my right. We crossed a tiny creek, the banks on both sides displayed hoof prints and tracks from what I presumed to be a vehicle the local cops had driven along here to check things out while seeking evidence.

They were in a quandary. The Chief of the town, one Parnell Hastings, hadn't been reticent to admit he had little to go on when we met in his office.

"I almost wish the doc had missed the smack on the head. We might have called it an accident and been done with it."

"Except for changing horses in mid-ride."

"Right." Hastings scratched his gray hair and shifted his not inconsiderable bulk in his chair. He was reluctant to have me messing about in his investigation. I had no more standing than did any ordinary citizen, especially with cops. Dentists get more slack than do private investigators. However, this private citizen had skills, experience and a rep. That plus the trails at this happy horsesh** ranch were again open. So here I was, a reluctant cowboy, banging my bottom on a hard unforgiving dish of leather, trying to find some clue to Springfield's demise. It had been my decision to ride out here via horse rather than on an ATV. Put me closer to the possible actual circumstances of the man's last experience. The problem at the moment was motive. If I could find that, I might deduce a killer. I also couldn't figure out the horse exchange. That made no sense.

Entering another grove of trees, oaks, I suspected, we passed under a leafy canopy, dappled by the sunlight streaming in from our right. I glanced at Catherine who was suddenly bending low over her horse's neck.

"What's the matter?" Sharp. Keenly observant, I am. Yoda, maybe.

"Some of these tree branches are pretty low."

"I guess my height is advantageous here, hey?"

We pulled up in the shade to let the horses munch some grass and leaves from the bushes beside the trail. I looked down at the ground. I considered leaping off Sally, but getting back on would have been somewhat humiliating. Catherine would have had to lift me so my left foot would hook into the shortened stirrup. Or we'd have had to find a stump for me to stand on. Next time I would insist on a smaller horse. Next time? Never happen.

"Lots of tracks, hoof prints here. Milling about, it looks like," I said.

"The trail leads straight through there," Catherine pointed. "But look at the edges of the clearing."

"Yeah, I noticed. At least one horse either came or went at about right angles to the main trail." I squinted at the undergrowth. "No trail there. But which horse? And why?"

"Sean, you can tell direction by the marks. The shoes on the horses are rounded at the front. A horseshoe forms a half-circle with the opening at the back. See? Some of them have distinctive shoe patterns." She pointed at the ground again.

"I get it. More usefully, I see it. A horse with the same kind of shoes went both ways through those bushes over there." I pointed and thought about it. "And the heavier the horse or the more weight it carries affects the depth of the marks."

"All else being equal."

"So in good tracking conditions, say damp sand, you might be able to tell if a particular horse was carrying a different weight going and then coming."

Catherine was following my rumination. "Other things."

I nodded. "Sure, like, is the horse walking, running, hopping or skipping."

"Hopping?"

"Yeah, you know, the fine art of horse hopping." Then I leaned way back in the saddle to sort of ease my buns. My horse, Sally, feeling my weight shift, I suppose, lifted her head and stepped to the left, crowding the bushes at the edge of the little clearing. She reached for an unmolested twig of young leaves. I felt other branches plucking at my blue jeans. Catherine's horse merely flicked its tail and continued to crunch grass and leaves. I leaned way back and looked up at the thick canopy of leafy tree branches overhead.

That's when I spied a white scar midst all that greenery.

In spite of what the authorities tell you, chance and luck often play a big part in solving crimes, along with persistence and savvy. That's not to denigrate the expertise and hard work of police people. Often lucky breaks come because of savvy and experience. If you are in the right place with the right attitude, luck and chance can take a hand. If my horse, Sally, hadn't moved aside that afternoon, just at a time when the sun was highlighting the branches overhead, and if I hadn't looked up into the canopy, the broken branch end might never have been seen. Of course, I was looking for anomalies.

"A branch was recently broken up there," I said, pointing.

Catherine backed her horse and squinted up. "I see it."

"Do you see any other recently broken branches?" We spent several moments peering up trying to locate other breaks. Nothing. "No recent wind storms out here in your recollection?" Another negative. By staring at the jagged end until my eyes watered and I got a crick in my neck, I was able to determine the approximate size and length of the piece that must have come off the tree. Catherine dismounted and at my direction went about the clearing and the bushes until she found several limp bits of oak leaf and twigs that had to have come off the branch in question.

"So what do you think?" She handed me several leaves.

"I think you are quite fetching in those tight riding pants. I also think someone could have obtained a cudgel by the simple expedient of breaking off a branch large enough to do the job, but small enough to be obtainable without the use of a saw. Which suggests to me that killing the councilman was not planned. We need to find that branch."

"The killer seized an opportunity out here?"

"Exactly. How much do we know about Springfield? I ask because it's possible he was killed over something that is not related to the eminent domain disagreement."

Catherine nodded. "Mr. Springfield has been involved in other controversy, I hear. Maybe we should go back to the barn so you can pursue those questions."

I smiled my agreement. "I like your way of thinking, but there are more questions out here. Why is there no missing horse and where is the branch that was a cudgel? Can we discover which horse came and which went?"

"This trail," my companion pointed, "leads to the highest place on the ranch. Let's go there and you can see a good deal of what else there is to be seen."

We did that. It took an additional twenty minutes and when we got there I saw what our problem was.

There was too damn much property. Great for those who wanted to ride in a relatively serene rural environment with open glades and wild critters. I spent several minutes scanning the property I could see from our vantage point. I was hoping to see a riderless horse. I didn't. That left only one alternative. We'd follow the single horse track away from the clearing behind us in the hope of learning something else relevant to the crime.

An hour later we ran out of tracks. I was pretty sure we were still following the same horse, but I wasn't sure the horse we were following had anything to do with the crime. A few yards farther on from the edge of a vast meadow where we stopped I saw a fence. There was brush all along it and beyond it I heard an automobile engine. There was a road there, a paved road.

"Look," I said. "Civilization. Must be the edge of the property."

"Or the edge of the world," grinned Catherine. One of the wonderful and attractive aspects of my girlfriend is that she often understands exactly how I am feeling at almost any given moment.

We stared around at the bucolic scene. I transferred my gaze to the ground in front of me. "In spite of the passage of two day's time, I believe that a horse went down this slope toward the road. Possibly carrying the killer."

"A great leap of hope," Catherine muttered.

We urged our mounts forward and while it was clear that Sally, at least, thought we should be going the other direction toward the barns, we sauntered down the gentle swale until we came up against the thick growth of bushes that hugged the fence line. Across the fence was a ditch and a two lane suburban road. The closer we approached the bushes, the more antsy the horses became. I looked around while patting Sally's broad brown neck. A few yards away was a stump of a tree. I urged Sally closer so I could dismount without having to sprawl on the ground.

"Take her reins, while I have a look around," I said. Catherine did so and walked both horses a way away until they calmed down a little. Something had alarmed the beasts and I intended to find out what.

Now that I was at ground level there were flies. Large black noisy flies that buzzed about my head and led me into the thicket.

The flies were attracted to a short tree branch entangled in the bushes. It was an ordinary branch of an oak tree, stripped of leaves and sporting a smudge of rusty color at the very end on one side. To me, it looked like dried blood. I backed out of the shrubbery and walked to the stump where Catherine met me.

I told her what I had discovered. "You have your cell phone. Call the Barres and the cops. I'm willing to bet the blood on the branch belongs to the councilman."

While we waited for the cops I did some hard thinking. There was enough evidence to my experienced and trained mind that

I was able to construct a possible scenario. Whoever murdered Councilman Springfield put him back on a horse, turned that nag loose, rode to this spot, dropped the murder weapon, then returned to the barn.

After the police came and I explained my theory, I remounted with a boost from a grinning cop and we cantered our way back to the murder grove where I took another look around. Now that I'd found the cudgel and honed my tracking skills, I thought I might read the ground and make some sense of it. That didn't work.

Back at the barns, I eased my sore body out of the saddle and tipped my hat to the wrangler. He and his buddy, called the swamper I learned, secured the horses in their stalls.

"So, find any evidence?" I thought the swamper seemed a mite eager.

"Where's the horse that carried the dead councilman back here?" I asked.

"Stall down there," said the wrangler. "Cops made us keep her in the barn after they decided it weren't no accident."

"Show me please." The swamper took me down the broad aisle between the box stalls.

We stopped half way down the barn and there was a sudden pounding of hooves. The dancing horse inside pricked its ears and backed away, looking at us. In the next stall, another horse munched calmly on some hay. I leaned on the stall gate and regarded the first animal. The swamper stepped back and indicated the horse I was looking at.

"This the horse he came back on?" I asked.

"Yep. So they said. I don't know one horse from another."

Then the swamper turned and brushed by me on his way back to the entrance to the barn. Whoa!

The first horse shied nervously, hooves pounded the floor.

Horses don't like the smell of blood and they don't like people who abuse them. This horse didn't like the swamper. Why?

"Hey," I called. Why doesn't this horse like you?"

The guy flinched, looked back at me and bolted for the barn door. Unfortunately, just as he pivoted out the entrance, with me in hot pursuit, another horse, one being unsaddled in the entrance, stepped to the side and slammed her rear into the guy. He bounced off the horse's rump, hit the side of the barn, and I was all over him.

Running in a horse barn is not a federal offense; escaping from a lockup can be. The dude was a fugitive from a jail near the councilman's lake place and he believed the councilman had recognized him. So he rode a horse hard to the grove and waylaid Springfield. After he killed the councilman, being unfamiliar with horses, he put the man on the wrong horse for the lonely ride back to the stable. Then he rode hard to conceal the branch and beat the dead body back to the barn. The horse remembered blood and hard handling by the swamper. It cost the man his freedom.

When the *St. Paul Pioneer Press* refused to pay for her little red convertible which was fire bombed while she covered a riot, Judith Yates Borger decided it was time to get a new gig. She began writing fiction and hasn't looked back on the decision. Borger draws on her 30 years experience as a journalist to chronicle the escapades of her protagonist Skeeter Hughes, wife, mom and reporter.

In real life, Borger is passionate about her work, her children, her grandchildren, and her marriage. She lives with her husband, John, and her dog, Honey, in downtown Minneapolis overlooking the Stone Arch Bridge on the Mississippi River, where she rows crew with the Minneapolis Rowing Club.

Be sure to visit her website, *www.JudithYatesBorger.com*

Stone Arch Bridge

Judith Yates Borger

She had never murdered anyone. Sure, she'd thought about it plenty of times, but just in the theoretical sort of way. Like her landlord when he doubled her rent. Occasionally she even thought about murdering her mother. But who doesn't think about that from time to time?

This was different. This was somebody who deserved to die.

Kate and Anna had been friends since kindergarten in Linden Hills. They met at the slide the first day of school when a boy tried to push Anna out of line. Kate came to her rescue, telling the boy in her loudest five-year-old voice to "stick it up your nose with a rubber hose." She had no idea what "it" was, but she knew it was something bad to say. From that day on, Anna looked up to Kate.

Anna and Kate giggled together in the back of Mrs. Corcoran's seventh-grade classroom when the meanest kid in the class returned from a bathroom break with a foot-long piece of toilet paper hanging from the back of his pants. They hugged and cried when four of their friends were killed in a car accident on prom night. After they left for college, Kate to the West Coast, Anna to the East Coast, they texted each other hundreds of times. After college, Kate got a job in Minneapolis as a financial analyst and bought a condo in the Warehouse District. Anna came home to Josh and a part-time job as a yoga instructor.

"He's a good catch," Anna said told Kate ten years later, just before they married. "He makes good money. He's charming and funny and cute."

"He's not funny when he drinks too much," Kate said as she and Anna shared a bottle of pinot noir. "He's thirty-two years old but he hasn't grown up. Not marriage material."

"This from the woman who knows all," Anna replied. "Josh and I have been together longer than your marriage lasted."

Kate wasn't convinced. She had to admit, however, that Josh and Anna looked like they were happy at first, although he was a little too involved with her decisions. He insisted on tagging along every time she went shopping. Still, he had great taste in women's clothes and they had a nice home with an honest-to-God picket fence in Edina.

One day Kate dropped by Anna's clapboard house without calling first. She knocked. She rang the doorbell. Then she knocked again, and waited. She pulled out her cell phone and was about to call when a shadow flitted across the door's peephole.

Anna cracked open the door. "What are you doing here?"

"You aren't returning my calls, texts or emails," Kate said.

"You called?"

Kate was shocked at the sight of the woman who came to the door. She didn't even look like Anna. Her hair was straggly, her expression flat and dull. She'd lost about fifteen pounds she could ill afford.

"Can I come in?" Kate asked.

After another wait, Anna stepped aside. The house with the pristine front yard was a wreck inside and smelled of beer and cigarettes.

"Where did you get that black eye?" Kate asked.

"I walked into a door," Anna replied.

Anna was a small woman, probably no more than a hundred pounds. Kate had no problem imagining that Josh had pounded Anna.

"You understand that I don't believe you, right?"

Anna nodded then headed for the kitchen, with Kate trailing behind. She opened a cupboard, took out a pack of Marlboros and lit up. Kate had never seen Anna smoke in all the years they had been friends.

Kate parked herself at Anna's kitchen table and looked around. Bread stuck up stiff from the toaster and the cat was licking dirty plates in the open dishwasher. Red sauce had spattered and dried on the wall next to the stove. Anna, apparently oblivious to the mess, pulled an empty can from the trash and set it down on the table to use as an ashtray. The combined smells of cigarette and residual cat food almost made Kate vomit, but she decided not to fight that battle with Anna. There were bigger issues.

"How did you get the black eye?" Kate asked.

"Walked into a door, I told you," Anna said.

"Come on," Kate said.

"Whatever." Anna waved her cigarette. "Wine?" she asked as she pulled a bottle from the fridge.

"Sure, thanks. You've got to leave Josh," Kate said.

"And go where?"

"There are lots of places," Kate said. "Harriet Tubman. The Sojourner Project."

"I don't want to leave my house," Anna said. "The neighbors will find out."

"Okay, then, kick him out."

"Tried that."

"And he left you with a black eye?"

Anna didn't say anything, just picked at the Sebastiani label on the pinot.

"Where am I going to get money?" Anna asked. "Teaching yoga is not exactly a high-paying job."

"I'll help you," Kate said.

"Well, isn't that special?" Anna said. "The big-deal professional woman is supporting her lost little friend."

Kate had never seen that flash of resentment in Anna's eyes or heard it in her voice before. She pulled back from the table.

"Fine. Then get a restraining order against the bastard. The pinot's gone and so am I."

The next day Kate chewed this matter over as she walked her white Shih Tzu, Fluffy, on the Stone Arch Bridge across the Mississippi River in Minneapolis. It was her best place to think. She loved the faint glow cast by the late eighteenth-century lamps that lined the bridge, where only walkers and bikers are allowed. Her favorite time of year was after the winter solstice when the sun was just setting. The light reminded her of a Prince poster, all deep purples and blues, which reminded her of the Prince concert she and Anna had gone to while they were home on break from college. She had been surprised when Anna lashed out at her, but she knew Anna didn't really mean what she said. Kate could never stay angry with sweet Anna.

Fluffy stopped to sniff a light pole when Kate came to a decision. She didn't believe she could even think such a thing. It was so rash, so absolute. So violent. But she knew it was the only way to keep Josh away from Anna.

Josh had to die.

Kate kept walking and thinking. She would have to come up with something cunning, something no one would be able to trace.

Kate stopped to look at the giant doors on the lock and dam at St. Anthony Falls. They reminded her of the huge gate that was supposed to keep King Kong in the jungle. Sure would like to see Josh crushed between those bad boys, she thought. But that would leave his body. Murder is harder for a woman than a man, she thought. First, there's the obvious difference in muscle mass, even though Josh was not much taller than Kate. Whacking him in the head is difficult when the sledgehammer, or whatever, is too heavy. A lighter tool is less effective. A bullet to the brain? Even if she could find a brain in that moron's head a gun was not an option. Kate had signed too many anti-gun petitions to even think about it. Besides, the thought of bone cracking, muscle tearing or tissue spilling from his head was too gruesome. Poison? Probably the easiest option, but that would leave a body and point to Anna as the killer. Kate didn't want to give her more trouble than she already had. She walked on.

While Fluffy stopped to pee, Kate turned the other way to admire the blue lighting under the 35W bridge, downstream less than a mile. Kate thought about Huck Finn rafting down the river with his friend, Jim. What an adventure that would be, all the way to the Gulf of Mexico. A sly smile spread across her face as she continued to walk. She would lure Josh to the icy bridge.

Over the next several weeks Kate followed Josh on Facebook. Every time he posted his location she would follow. Brooks Brothers. Haskell's. Surdyk's. She watched him carefully, sometimes from afar, researching his habits. Then one day in France 44 Liquors, her shopping cart just happened to bump into his.

"Hey," she said as the bottles in both their carts clinked together.

"Hey yourself," he said, throwing her a big, beautiful smile.

"Stocking up?"

All of a sudden, Kate saw what Anna found attractive about Josh. No question he was cute, with blond curly hair and big brown eyes. He spent money like a man who has plenty. But it was more than that. His deep voice rumbled like thunder in the distance. He had an air of confidence about him, a surety that fueled a magnetic force.

"What are you going to do with all that liquor?" he asked.

"I might ask you the same," she replied.

They bantered back and forth like tennis players anticipating each other's moves. Kate invited Josh back to her condo. She had planned to seduce him into a drunken stupor, then complete her plan to kill him.

Instead, he seduced her.

Soon they were meeting two, three times a week, always at Kate's place. "Anna's got a restraining order against me," Josh said. "I can't go home." Their evenings were full of boozy lovemaking. They talked. They laughed. They danced

"Did you give Anna that black eye?" Kate asked Josh one evening.

"No. She ran into a door."

"I've heard that before," Kate said. "We both know that's a euphemism."

"It's what happened," Josh said. "I never touched her. If I had hurt her, wouldn't I have hurt you by now?"

"But I saw her," Kate said. "She looked terrible."

"I don't know what's happened to her. She's not the woman I married. She's changed. She's ..." Josh's voice trailed off.

Kate knew he had a point. Josh never so much as raised a finger to hurt her. She just couldn't believe he would beat Anna, which made her furious. With Anna. How could she say those things about Josh that were so mean? So untrue? It was Anna who had the problem, not Josh. Kate decided she needed to question Anna.

"Let's go for a walk," Kate said to Anna.

"Where?"

"The Stone Arch Bridge."

And so that's where they were, on an icy evening in December just after the winter solstice, strolling across the bridge, with Fluffy.

"Why did you tell me Josh hurt you?" Kate asked.

"I didn't. I told you I walked into a door," Anna replied.

"Yeah, that's right," Kate said.

Snow started to fall in clumps, sticking to the thin ice on the river below the bridge. Kate always loved that pattern. It reminded her of bridal lace.

They made no sound in their Uggs as they trudged across the bridge. About half way, Anna stepped up on the curb and leaned over the railing, looking downriver toward the 35W bridge. The strings from the earflaps on her red knit hat dangled high above the water. Kate leaned on the bridge rail, too. They both stared at the water for a while, until Anna turned to Kate, tears in her eyes, snot dripping from her bright red nose.

"I'm embarrassed." She wiped her nose with a matted tissue full of lint. "You have a great life, a good job, a cool place to live. You go out all the time. I'm stuck with a husband who beats me."

"You're lying," Kate said. "Somebody hurt you, but it wasn't Josh."

"How do you know?"

"Because I love him. He has never hurt me and I know he wouldn't hurt you."

"YOU love him?" Anna asked.

"Yes."

"He's a bastard," Anna said.

"He's a good man," Kate said. "You told me yourself. He's charming and funny and cute."

"No," Anna said. "He *uses* women."

Anna was incensed. Her breath came out of her mouth like puffs from the smokestack on the river's bank. How could Kate be so stupid, Anna wondered to herself. How could Kate, Anna's best friend, who had everything Anna ever wanted, take the only thing Anna had, her man?

Anna bent down to pet Fluffy, sitting patiently below the curb. As she pressed her face into the warm, soft fur she had an epiphany.

She grabbed Kate's feet and stood up fast, catching her off guard. Kate gave out a quick scream and grabbed the guardrail, but her mittens made her grip slippery.

"What are you doing?" she asked Anna. "This isn't funny."

"No, it's not funny," Anna said. "Josh is a bastard, but he's *my* bastard.

Kate landed a hard kick on Anna's chin, but Anna was un-daunted. Using the core power she had built through yoga, Anna flipped Kate over the side of the bridge. Thin ice below broke into tiny shards as the steely grey river grabbed Kate, pulling her under and away in a rush of water before she had time to scream. The last Anna saw of Kate was her face looking up at her in shock. Kate was gone, Anna thought, all the way to the Gulf of Mexico.

Anna tossed her dirty tissue into the river and waved her fingers.

Joel Arnold lives in Savage, Minnesota with his wife, two kids, two cats, a dog and a rat. His writing has appeared in over sixty publications, including *Weird Tales*, the anthologies *Resort to Murder* and *Writes of Spring, American Road Magazine* and *Cat Fancy*. He collects old typewriters and loves to drive the back roads of America looking for all things quirky.

All of his short story collections, as well as four novels, are available in ebook format. His horror novel, *Northwoods Deep*, and his young adult historical novel, *Ox Cart Angel*, are available in trade paperback. In 2010, Joel received both a Gulliver Travel and Research Grant and a Minnesota Artist Initiative Grant.

Joel keeps a blog at **http://authorjoelarnold.blogspot.com**, and can be found on Facebook at **www.facebook.com/#!/AuthorJoelArnold**. He'd love to hear from you.

Look for his debut mystery novel *Licking the Marmot*, which takes place among the employees of Yellowstone National Park, coming soon!

Blue-Eyed Mary

Joel Arnold

There's a group of sandstone caves in Rochester near the top of what is now a public park called Quarry Hill. The caves were carved out in 1882 by inmates of the Second Minnesota Asylum for the Insane, led by a man named Thomas Coyne.

At one point, Coyne, a schizophrenic who believed he was Jesus Christ, carved the words to an old song on one of the cave walls, and although faded, they can still be made out to this day:

Come tell me blue-eyed stranger, say whither dost thou roam?
O'er this wide world a ranger, has thou no friends or home?
They called me blue-eyed Mary when friends and fortune
                                        smiled,
But says blue-eyed Mary, now I am sorrow's child.

Today, the cave entrances are blocked by iron, padlocked gates, but it wasn't long ago that they were open to anyone curious enough to enter. Teenagers hiked up to them after dark to get wasted, make out, or have a good scare. I know of at least two children conceived within those dark cave walls, but it wasn't until this year that I knew their names.

And I will confess right here and now to killing one of them.

Five months ago I balanced a tuna hotdish in one hand and a bouquet of daisies in the other as I pressed the doorbell to my mother's house with my elbow. After a minute, I rang it again, the casserole dish hot on my palm. I'd only called fifteen minutes earlier from home and knew she was expecting me. When she still didn't answer, I set the daisies down and tried the door. Unlocked. I entered, about to call out *Mom*, but saw her on the couch, crying. The only other time I'd seen her crying was when Dad died, and that had been over thirty years ago.

"What is it?" I asked.

There was the usual fragrance of orange and cloves; she still made the same pomanders that she did when I was a kid. I set the hotdish on her dining room table, forgetting about the daisies outside the door. Something fluttered in my stomach. "What's wrong?" *Cancer? A brain tumor?*

She shook her head.

I leaned down and gave her a hug. "Come on. What is it?" I wiped at her tears with my knuckles.

She swallowed. "The news," she said, nodding at the television. "There was a story…"

"About what?"

She picked up the remote and pressed the reverse button for the DVR. Images sped backward through a set of commercials and a portion of the evening news. "Here," she said. "This."

It was a story about the St. Paul Catholic Infants Home, an orphanage that also served as a home where young, unwed mothers went in secret to deliver their babies. It was known as Watermelon Hill by the local youth who thought the young women going in and out of the building looked like they carried watermelons under their dresses.

"I was one of those girls," Mom said. "My parents sent me there when I was seventeen. I was five months pregnant."

Although I'd grown up an only child, I knew I wasn't *that* particular watermelon. I asked stupidly, "Did Dad know?"

Mom shrugged. "I told him on our second date that I'd had a baby, but I didn't go into the details. He didn't seem to want them."

My father, Conrad Gordon, died of a self-inflicted gunshot in 1980. I was barely eight years old. He checked into a motel room with only a gun wrapped in a towel stuffed in a briefcase. A maid found his body. At the time, I was told it was a heart attack; I wasn't told it was suicide until I was sixteen. Mom showed me the gun, a Ruger Security-Six. I remember touching it, but I never asked her why she'd kept it.

"What happened to the baby?" I asked.

Mom shook her head, fresh tears brimming. "They swaddled her up and let me hold her for a few moments before making me give her back. They told me it was for the best." Mom tried valiantly to smile through her tears. "She had such beautiful blue eyes. I'd carried her all those months, and that was all I got."

"I can't imagine how hard that must've been."

"It was the hardest thing in my life."

"Whatever happened to her?"

Mom shrugged. "I don't know. Adopted, probably. That's what happened to those children." She looked at me and patted my hand. "But then I had you. You are the joy of my life, and that what's important."

We sat down to the tuna hotdish. There were so many questions to ask. So many that I ended up not asking any at all. Not until later.

This morning, a high school senior found the body. He lived near Quarry Hill, and, on early Saturday mornings, he'd bring his alto sax to the edge of the old, abandoned quarry below the caves and play jazz. He told the news reporter that he liked the acoustics of the place, the way the notes echoed off the limestone walls. He liked to watch the sun rise over the hill, and told the reporter that he didn't notice anything wrong until the sun crested the hill. Then he saw something in the old blasting shack on the quarry floor. He went down to check it out and found a body slumped down in the shack, a leather jacket covering the head and shoulders.

I don't know how early the kid arrived at the quarry, but he probably didn't miss me by much.

It was impossible to stop thinking about what my mom went through as a teenager and how she'd kept it a secret for so many years. But most of all, I couldn't stop thinking that I had a sibling out there. Was she still alive? Did she know she was adopted? Would I meet her someday?

Not long after learning of my new sibling, I stopped by Mom's for a visit, armed with a bottle of her favorite white wine. I wanted information.

I pulled the cork and poured her a glass. She always kept a sixpack of beer for me in the fridge, so I grabbed a can and sat next to her on the couch.

"I don't really know how to ask this, but I can't help but wonder if that half-sister of mine is out there somewhere," I said.

Mom tensed as she sipped her wine. I guzzled half my beer and plunged head. "I want to find her."

She shook her head. "That's not a question."

I took a deep breath before finally asking, "May I have your permission to find her?"

It was Mom's turn to sigh. She rubbed her temples and closed her eyes. She took a long sip of wine, finishing off her glass. As I poured her another, she said, "She was my blue-eyed Mary long before I gave birth to her. That's what I'd call her when I talked to her in the womb."

"You knew she was a girl *before* she was born?"

She looked up at me, her eyes bright and wet. "I can't tell you how I knew, but I knew. I could picture her. And when I finally saw those blue eyes, I knew I was right. We had this special connection. Even after they took her away, even after it seemed like a part of me died, I still *felt* her."

"But you never found out what happened to her? Where she went? If she's even still alive?"

She patted my forearm. "Before you were born, I still felt that connection. I felt I knew what she looked like, what she was doing, what her voice sounded like, what her moods were. Of course, when you came along, you took my full attention, but I still…*felt* her. My blue-eyed Mary. And yes, I feel that she's alive somewhere."

My spirits rose. "Let's find her," I said. "The both of us."

She shook her head. "I don't think I want her to know me."

"Why?"

"What if she had a bad life? It would be my fault, wouldn't it?"

"You were seventeen," I said. "A kid. Nobody's going to pass judgment on you *now*." I thought for a moment. "How old would she be?"

She didn't even need to think about it. "Forty-six."

"What if I can find her? "

"It was a closed adoption, Michael. They don't just give that information out to anyone."

"Can I at least try?"

Mom looked at me, her eyes warm and sympathetic. "I just

don't know if it's a good idea." She managed a smile and shrugged. "But I won't tell you no."

I wrote a letter to the Catholic Charities in St. Paul requesting information. I also sent a letter to be placed in the adoptee's file, a way to let the adoptee know that the birth mother was open for contact. Of course, I wrote it all in my mother's name, Donna Gordon, and put her return address on it so that any information would go right to her.

So when Mom called me a month ago and said, "I got something in the mail," I knew what she was talking about.

"I'll be right over."

Mom still lives in the same house I grew up in. Not much has changed, save for the framed photographs in the hallway where you can watch me grow up. Even then, the newest picture is from my college graduation over fifteen years ago. Once, before she retired from Mayo, I took the day off from work and spent it painting her living room. I thought the white walls could use an update, so I laid down a base coat first thing in the morning and spent the rest of the day adding a darker coat of taupe, daubing it with a rag to give it a faux-leather look. Tedious work, but I managed to finish just before she got home.

When she came through the door and saw me splotched with paint, she gasped and raised her hand to her mouth. It was like she'd just seen someone get hit by a bus.

"Surprise!" I said.

When I came for dinner two weeks later, the walls were back to white. She made no mention of it as she poked holes in an orange and filled them with cloves.

You think I would've learned.

But that day the letter arrived...

"I'm afraid to open it," she said.

I turned the envelope over in my hands. "We can't *not* open it." It was addressed by hand, the return address had the surname *Billings* with a Milwaukee address. I slid my finger under the envelope's flap, and paused slightly before pulling out the sheet of paper, waiting for Mom to object.

She sighed and shrugged. "Well?"

I unfolded the sheet of paper and read the handwritten letter. It was short and sweet.

Dear Donna,
Thanks for expressing interest in contacting me. I've been hoping for a long time that I might hear from you...
It went on for a bit longer, but...
"There must be some mistake."
Mom looked up. "What do you mean?"
This time I read the letter out loud to her, and when I got to the end, I read, *"Sincerely, Kent Michael Billings."*
Mom looked up. "What?"
"Kent Michael Billings," I said. "I'm guessing that's not a girl." Then I asked, "You *did* see her, didn't you? You're sure you had a *girl?*"
Mom reached for the letter and took it from my hand. Then she did something I was not expecting. She tore the letter into pieces. "I didn't have to see her. I knew. I always knew. It was a girl. And oh, such blue eyes. I wish you would've seen them, Michael."
So. Mom never *really* knew, did she?
Sometimes when you build up something so much in your mind...I realized that it had to be hard for her to accept that she'd had a son, not a daughter, but she'd come around eventually. And more important to me, *I had a brother out there!* And he lived in Milwaukee! An easy day's drive.
Growing up, I'd always wished for a brother, and even now, at thirty-eight years old, the idea of finding a long-lost brother was so...*exciting*.
Mom would come around.

I talked to him on the phone three weeks ago. He was just as excited as I was to find out he had a brother. He said he'd felt as if something like this might happen someday. And to think, his middle name was my first name!
Kent was twice divorced. No kids. Yes, he'd always known he was adopted. No, his parents never kept it a secret from him. More importantly, his parents were always good to him. Unfortunately, they were hit and killed by a drunk driver while he was attending

his junior year at college.

The last thing I'll tell you about our conversation is that deep, deep down, he always felt he had a brother somewhere. We talked for over an hour, but here's the thing—I want to keep the rest of our conversation private. Because it's all I really have left of this newfound brother of mine.

The only other time I heard Kent's voice was when he checked into the hotel on the outskirts of Rochester on Thursday night and called to say he'd made it in safely. He was nervous, but looking forward to finally meeting me and his birth mother in person on Friday night.

Last night it was all over the news. The unidentified body found in Quarry Hill Park by the high school senior. All they knew was that it was a male in his 40s or 50s. He had no identification on him. The police asked for any information that might help identify the victim.

What they didn't say on the news that night was that the gunshot wound that killed him had obliterated his face so that their sketch artist couldn't even do a rendering of the man.

I turned off Mom's television and turned to face her. Tears flowed freely from my eyes. I put my arms around her. Squeezed her so tight.

"Michael? Honey? What is it? What's wrong?"

Two weeks ago I tried to convince her to just meet with him. He was so eager to meet *her*.

"I really don't want to talk about it," she said.

"But, Mom, he doesn't blame you. He's had a good life, and, if anything, he's thankful that you gave him to such wonderful parents."

"I didn't give him to anybody. The nuns took my baby. *They* gave my baby away."

"You know what I mean," I said, exasperated.

She whirled around and stuck her finger in my face. "Listen to me," she said through gritted teeth. "I was raped in those caves."

I felt like I'd been slapped.

She stepped back, exhaling, and brushed away some imaginary lint from my shoulder. She lowered her voice. "I'm only going to tell you this once."

She told me how the boy she was dating all those years ago, Hank Beaumont, was tired of only getting to second base, and one night he took her up to the caves in Quarry Hill. Donna laid a blanket down on the dirt floor and Hank turned off his flashlight. They made out, their hands all over each other, but when Hank pleaded with her to go further, Donna refused.

"Please?" he begged. "Just this once?"

Donna said no, but Hank Beaumont didn't take no for an answer that night in the caves of Quarry Hill. He pinned her down with the weight of his body.

"Afterward, he found his flashlight and turned it on, setting it on the ground so that it pointed at the ceiling. He got dressed quickly and told me to hurry up. I was hurt. Bleeding. I couldn't stop crying. I begged him to go and leave me alone. I couldn't look at him. I got dressed facing the cave wall, and that's when I noticed the words carved there. A poem. I ran my fingers over them and read them in the dim light.

> 'Come tell me blue-eyed stranger, say whither dost thou roam?
> O'er this wide world a ranger, hast thou no friends or home?
> They called me blue-eyed Mary when friends and fortune
> smiled.
> But says blue-eyed Mary, now I am sorrow's child.'

"It was signed 'Coyne the Prophet.' At that moment, I thought he was talking directly at me, as if I was Blue-Eyed Mary. But I realized later that it wasn't me. It was the baby that started forming inside me that night."

Sometime early Saturday morning, a few hours before dawn, I drove up to the Quarry Hill picnic shelter with my lights off, following the glow of the half moon. The shelter was surrounded by trees, and there was no one else there. I parked as close to the trail that led to the caves as possible.

My half-brother was heavy. I dragged him a bit at a time,

resting often. The sound of his shoes sliding on the dry autumn leaves on the wide trail seemed unbelievably loud; I felt like the whole city could hear us.

I intended to place him in the cave, under the verse chiseled into the wall by Thomas Coyne. *Coyne the Prophet.* But as I neared the cave's entrance, I discovered that it was closed, a locked iron gate placed across its mouth.

I was exhausted. I looked out over the quarry spread below me, the half-moon painting the limestone a dull gray. It would have to do. I steeled myself, whispered to his lifeless body, "I'm sorry, brother," and began to drag him once again.

But I'm getting ahead of myself.

Friday night I sat at a table in a restaurant in downtown Rochester. Kent Michael Billings was supposed to meet Mom at her home and have some time to get to know each other. Then they were to meet me here at seven. I checked my watch. It was now just past eight.

I called Mom's house, but got her voice mail. I ordered another beer and nursed it for another hour. Still no Mom. No Kent, no long-lost brother. I paid the bill and left. Maybe, I thought, they were so caught up in each other's stories that they'd forgotten the time.

Or maybe something was wrong.

I tried calling one more time, to no avail. I drove to her house. When I rang, the bell my mother opened the door.

"Where's Kent?" I asked.

I smelled oranges and cloves.

Mom shook her head. "Who?"

"What do you mean, *who?* Where's Kent?"

"I'm here by myself," Mom said. "I was hoping you'd stop by."

I stared at her a moment before pushing myself past her into the house. "Did he call?"

"Nobody called," Mom said.

"He didn't call? Did you try the hotel?"

"What are you talking about?"

I grabbed my mother's shoulders. "Come on—don't do this to me. *Kent,*" I said. "Where is *Kent?* Your son?"

Mom reached up and brushed a strand of hair from my forehead. "You've always been my one and only son, and always will be. You know that."

There was blood on my mother's fingers. "What is going on? What happened to your fingers?"

She held up her hands and examined them. "I guess I got carried away with my pomanders. Those cloves can be sharp little buggers."

I walked past her into the kitchen. Where were these pomanders, these oranges and cloves that I smelled so acutely?

And just where the hell was my brother?

"Kent," I said again to my mother as I walked past her. "Let's stay on subject. Kent. The son you had forty-six years ago. The brother I invited here to meet us. Come *on*, Mom. This isn't funny."

I stood at the top of the basement steps. The oranges and cloves smell seemed to come from down there, but there was another scent that I couldn't quite place. It was like a piece of burnt toast, or...I couldn't place it. I hurried down the steps.

Dozens of oranges were set on the basement shelves, each orange studded with cloves.

Then I noticed my father's Ruger lying on the dark, shag carpet. That's what I had smelled—the discharge of a gun.

I faced the back of my dad's old easy chair six feet away from me. I noticed a hand on the armrest.

Oh, God. No.

I took three quick steps toward the chair and braced myself before looking down. It was Kent. Most of his face was gone, but I knew it was him—my long lost brother.

I felt someone behind me.

"A stranger," Mom said. "He knocked on the door, and I answered, and he walked right in. I had Conrad's gun. I'd been looking at it earlier. I don't know why, but I had it with me. He tried to talk to me, tell me things. Things I didn't want to hear."

"*Mom.*"

"He kept talking."

"*Mom,*" I repeated.

"He's a *stranger.* He's *not* my blue-eyed Mary. He's a *stranger,* don't you see?"

"Oh, God, *Mom*."

I barely caught her as she collapsed in my arms, sobbing. I held her.

"Okay," I said, patting her back. "We'll figure this out. We'll take care of it."

"*You're* my son," she cried. "You're my only son."

"Okay, okay," I soothed. When she felt steady enough, I eased her down onto a wooden chair. I picked the Ruger carefully up off the floor, emptied out the bullets, and put them in my pocket. Then I found a bottle of white wine. "You go upstairs," I said, handing it to her. "Pour yourself a glass. I'll take care of..." I couldn't finish the sentence.

My brother.

I began to clean up, trying to think of the best way to deal with the situation. Maybe not the best way, but the *only* way that I thought possible.

Saturday, sometime before dawn as I dragged my brother down the path into the quarry, I realized that my mother had built up her first child in her mind so much, her blue-eyed Mary; she knew her, created her out of pain, regret, guilt, sorrow...*necessity*. She had tried to create something that might turn that night in the caves and all those days at Watermelon Hill into something... *good*.

I told you that I murdered one of two children conceived in the caves of Quarry Hill.

I murdered *her*, murdered my mother's blue-eyed Mary. I murdered her by finding my mother's real child. Her other boy. Kent Michael Billings. The man I now dragged in starts and stops down to the old quarry floor. He deserved better than this. I know that. But I didn't know what else to do.

I placed Kent in the old blasting shack, a small closet-sized building of crumbling limestone. At least, I thought, it would protect him from the elements. I placed his leather jacket over his head. It seemed like the decent thing to do.

I thought about a lot of things that night, things about my father's death, suspicions that I'll never share with anybody.

I did my best to cover my tracks, but I'm sure I missed

something. Seems like you can't even blink without some forensic lab finding out about it. But that's okay. If they connect the murder to us, I'll confess to this one, too. I'll confess that it was me and me alone who shot Kent Michael Billings. It's what an only son does for his mother.